The Final Offering

This is a work of fiction. All of the characters are fictitious, and any resemblance to real coincidental.

THE FINAL OFFERING

Copyright © 2016 J.G. Gatewood

A J.G. Gatewood Book

www.jggatewood.com

The Final Offering

Contents

Chapter 1	7
Chapter 2	19
Chapter 3	27
Chapter 4	37
Chapter 5	47
Chapter 6	55
Chapter 7	61
Chapter 8	69
Chapter 9	79
Chapter 10	85
Chapter 11	93
Chapter 12	101
Chapter 13	109
Chapter 14	119
Chapter 15	129
Chapter 16	139
Chapter 17	149
Chapter 18	155
Chapter 19	163
Chapter 1	171

Chapter 2 179
Chapter 3 185
Chapter 4 189
Chapter 5 197
Chapter 6 209
Chapter 7 219
Chapter 8 227
Chapter 9 235
Chapter 10 243
Chapter 11 249
Chapter 12 257
Chapter 13 263
Chapter 14 269
Chapter 15 275
Chapter 16 281
Chapter 17 291

The Final Offering

This book is dedicated to my beautiful wife, Sarah. I only hope I've given enough life to capture what you were thinking. Thank you for all you do for me, including the countless edits. This story wouldn't be what it is without you.

The Final Offering

Part I – A Breach of the Contract

Chapter 1

Thula heard arguing in the common square of the village while dressing for the day. The quiet voices were hard to make out, but the anger was clear. With a quick check in the mirror to make sure she was presentable, she ran outside to find the source of all the commotion. Not that she cared about her appearance—she wasn't one of "those" fairies—but she wanted to look decent.

Many of the older members of the community stood outside the governor's home, yelling in gruff voices for a move to action. Her bright green eyes surveyed the scene, and her muscles tensed under her dark, brown skin.

She listened with tall pointy ears in disbelief.

"You're going to stand back and let this happen?"

"You're a coward!"

"This is an invasion of our territory. We must act!"

The Haloti have always been a peaceful people, she thought. *Why is everyone so irate? What is going on?*

A strong breeze ruffled her light brown hair, revealing the faint traces of the tattoos climbing her neck. Eager for them to make their full appearance, it would be at least another year before it would happen. The anger in the crowd grew. She fluttered her small translucent wings with unease while Governor Linotas spoke to the crowd.

The wind rippled the governor's flowing, green honorary robes of silk, and Thula held her breath in anticipation. His old and leathery face complemented his wise, brown eyes. Judging by the gray hair held back in a ponytail, and loose hanging mustachios, one could sense his age. His hair was in sharp contrast to his dark skin.

Thula strode along the gray branch, searching for a friendly face. The rough textures felt good underneath her feet, it was sturdy and familiar. The sound of the various birds chirping about and the squirrels playing tag back and forth brought her comfort.

Amridon, her best friend, stood behind several elders and she stood next to him. "What is all this?"

His eyes lit up like a candle and a smile spread across his lips. "Thula, about time you found us." He looked at the bright sky, staring at the sun. "Slept a little late, didn't you?"

"I was tired and had nothing important requiring my attention this morning." Her eyes followed his to the sky, and a gasp left her lips. How was the sun so close to its pinnacle? It was almost lunchtime. "It isn't any of your business what I do anyway."

Amridon's attention shifted to the governor. "Can you believe this has happened? I mean we've heard about them since we were children, but I never expected anything like this."

Noticing the gathering of villagers, she asked, "Believe what? I don't understand what's happening."

The Final Offering

"Oh, you did oversleep, didn't you?" he asked. "I was only kidding before, but a scout found a Grimmox last night in our part of the tree. Up here, Thula," he said, visibly mortified by just the thought. "They know better than to venture outside their territory. It's part of the treaty. They stay on the bottom, and we stay on the top."

The anger in his voice wasn't lost on her, but she had no idea how to respond. *I can't believe it. Why would they risk generations of peace?* Growing up as a Haloti, she had heard all the stories, but there had to be a logical explanation. The Grimmox couldn't be as bad as their histories painted them to be, could they? *How can we be afraid of something we don't understand?* She stiffened, against the dire news, and if truth be told, she didn't care for the conviction Amridon already held for the entire Grimmox population

"Are you sure? Who saw it?" she asked.

"It was a younger soldier on patrol. He found it spying on our village."

"How can we be sure? We haven't seen a Grimmox in several generations. How did the soldier even know what one looks like?"

Why does everyone always assume the worst? It's not as though the Grimmox tried attacking us.

"Why does it matter? Shouldn't you be more upset about this? You should want vengeance just as much as I do. If this soldier claims to have seen one, then I don't doubt him," he said. "Besides, you can't tell me you wouldn't love an opportunity to put an arrow into the chest of one of those beasts? Just imagine if we took the fight to them, there would be no more offering. We could live a life free from that curse; we wouldn't have to fear for our children." His voice and eyes implored her.

"We both know how bad the offering is. I detest it as much as you do, but it's part of our culture. Even if we lose one of our own every year, it's not worth starting a war. I understand the risks as much as anyone else." She sighed.

"Thula, I have one more year, but you still have two. I don't think I can live with myself if you are chosen." His gaze fell on the branch and he kicked at it.

"I'm afraid of the offering too," she said, stepping closer and placing a hand on his chest. "But it's not something I'll waste my time worrying about."

"No, I won't accept that. I don't want to worry about it. We need to put a stop to it right now before we risk any more souls to an antiquated ritual. I'd stand with my brethren to protect what is ours. Can't you see how important this is?"

Thula furrowed her brow in frustration. Yes, she could see that it was very important to him, but she didn't want to accept his words. She wouldn't accept his words. *Why does he have to be so hard headed?*

"Are you that eager to start a war? I've always respected your level head and ability to stay calm in tight situations. You must see that the costs are more than the possible benefits." she said. *How can he be so foolish?* She wondered.

Amridon scoffed. "Come now. I don't want to start a war, but if given the opportunity I'll do my part to protect all we hold dear." He walked up and put his arm around her, wearing a look in his eyes that showed his arrogance.

She almost flinched at his touch. Something seemed different about him, and she didn't like the aggressive nature he adopted; his words seemed empty and hollow. Then again, perhaps she was being ridiculous. Emotions were running high right now. Amridon's would be no different. She calmed down,

The Final Offering

welcoming his embrace. "Do you really think this will lead to a war?" she asked.

"I doubt it. I'm sure we're just bothered by the sighting. I'm confident it'll all work out just fine." It sounded as if he were placating her, while at the same time hoping for a chance to prove his prowess.

Rather than continuing their argument, she refocused her attention on the governor as he continued speaking.

"Look, I understand your frustration and I'm just as startled by this revelation, but we need to be careful and gather the evidence before we move ahead." The governor took a deep breath before continuing. "I won't risk a war with the Grimmox over rumors. We have stuck by our end of the treaty by continuing with the absurd tradition of the offering. The Grimmox have honored their end by leaving us alone and letting us live our lives as we see fit. I have a hard time accepting they would risk centuries of peace by spying on us, and to what end?" His lips spread into a smile and to Thula, he looked confident in his words.

More grumblings rose from the crowd of Haloti citizens. Thula spotted her parents standing on the outskirts of the gathering. An older Haloti voiced his displeasure with the governor. "They have already broken the treaty by venturing so far north. Shouldn't there be retaliation on our part?" Others around them urged him to continue. "I won't risk the life of my child for the offering to a species who cannot be trusted." Others seconded his opinions and offered their own thoughts.

The governor waved his hands downward urging his citizens to remain calm. "I can see your displeasure and will speak with the council before I issue our next actions. Until then, we're getting nowhere. Take time and talk to your families. Let cooler heads prevail, and I'm sure we'll have a message for you later today."

To Thula, it seemed this wasn't what the crowd wanted to hear, and the governor drew the ire of many. Deep down she wanted him to say more, anything that would help explain his thoughts, but instead, he retreated into his own quarters, amidst anger and boos from the crowd.

She caught her father's attention from the opposite side of the branch and beckoned him to join her.

They both gave somewhat tremulous smiles as they walked over to meet them. Her father spoke first. "Amridon, Thula, what a pleasure to see you both this morning. Quite the speech, don't you think?" He pointed at the governor's home behind him and adopted a rigid posture, clearly upset by the words of the governor.

Thula registered the beautiful contrast in her parents' physical attributes. Her father had loose, dark hair framing his old and aged face. The many years of hard work showed in his muscular build and the various scars accrued with pride were on abundant display at all times. She would always hide a tender smirk, though, while thinking of this bear of a fairy spreading his warmth during scary storms that rocked their beloved tree, or his devoted attendance at little fairy's tea parties.

Just the same, Cellomes, she noted, was his exact opposite in both appearance and demeanor. With smooth skin, bright blue eyes, and flowing brown hair, they looked the odd pair. Especially considering his height was above average, and she stood a full head shorter. However, to all that knew them, they fit perfectly, balancing one another with effortless grace. Thula thought Gorven's disposition tended toward the passionate and boisterous, while her mother was always calmer and more inclined to use reason and sensibility.

The Final Offering

Thula brought herself back to the moment as Amridon said, "I was just arguing with your daughter who seems to have a different idea." She started to speak, but he interrupted her. "I guess I should know better by now," he said with a laugh.

Even though it shouldn't matter, his words hurt Thula and she looked away before she risked another argument.

"She's always been that way, so I understand what you mean," Gorven grinned. He looked at the crowd before speaking again. "If you don't mind, Thula, your mother and I have matters to attend to, but I want to have an extended conversation concerning the Grimmox. You're too important to risk to another offering. Maybe it's time we did something about it."

Thula nodded. "But I won't start a war over the issue. I've always loved you for your compassion so hopefully, it won't come to that. I'd love to hear your ideas because I don't know how I should react."

"But something has to be done, and if the governor won't do anything, maybe we will." Thula tried to continue the conversation, but her father waved her off. "We'll discuss this later. This isn't the time, nor is it the place." Without uttering another word, her parents turned and walked back to their home. Her mother offered one last glance and shrugged, indicating she didn't know what Gorven had in mind either.

Thula understood what her father was saying without speaking a word. She turned and spoke to Amridon. "I want to clear my head. It was great seeing you this morning," she said as her parents disappeared from sight and she started walking away.

"I can go with you."

"As much as I'd enjoy time with you, I'd like to be alone to gather my thoughts. This whole Grimmox situation has my stomach in knots."

Amridon frowned. "Very well, happy hunting," he said.

She turned and walked away as frustration coursed through her veins. *How does he know I'm going hunting?* She wondered. Then again, what else would she do? She was sometimes too predictable.

After grabbing her bow and donning a simple tunic made of silk, she set out on her hunt. The afternoon air was warm and thick, with the slightest hint of moisture. It had been dry the past several days, and she welcomed a little rain. The leaves of the tree were a bright green and yellow and she brushed her hands over the rough edges as she walked. They were sharp and would cut into her skin, but something in their touch helped to cleanse her soul. She was relaxed and refreshed for the first time all day. Several birds chirped on the branches above her head. Letting out a series of whistles, she tried to mimic their call, but she had never been good with the songs of the birds, and all she did was startle them. They took off into the sky and she seemed all alone.

As the day neared afternoon, she moved with stealth down a branch seeking cover behind several leaves as she moved closer to her prey. The rough bark under her feet offered her comfort and more than a little traction. A soft breeze brushed past her face and brought with it the scents of nature. She spotted a black caterpillar earlier with a red band of color through its midsection. Per Haloti laws, caterpillars were not to be touched. Many would one day turn into butterflies, but they also produced silk. This one though would turn into a moth, meaning she was free to pursue it.

The morning's worrisome scene still bothered her and she tried her best to put the thoughts out of her mind. Crouched behind a leaf, she tried to control her excitement. Adrenaline coursed through her body and her heart rate ran high—her heart

The Final Offering

pounded in her chest. She took a deep breath and closed her eyes to steady herself. Her father's lessons ran through her head and she listened to him issuing orders in his gruff voice. *Take a deep breath, pull back on the bow, steady your heartbeat.* The words brought a chuckle to her throat. She opened her eyes and peered around a jagged edge of the leaf. The caterpillar stopped about one-hundred paces down the bough as it encountered a rough knot jutting up in its path.

Her heartbeat quickened when she saw a bird several branches higher in the tree. It had its eye on the caterpillar too, and timing was of the essence. If she waited too long, she would lose her opportunity. Too quickly, and she would miss the target. She had to do it right the first time.

With an arrow nocked to her bow, she pulled back on the string. With one last deep breath, she calmed herself before letting it loose. It flew straight and whistled through the air as it turned into a blur and found its target. She fired several more at the creature in rapid succession to make sure it didn't suffer. The muscles contracted and the front end climbed into the air. Yellow fluid leaked from its many wounds before it crashed back down on the hard gray surface of the branch. Running to the creature's side and checking to make sure it was dead, she pumped her fist toward the bird who seemed no longer interested and flew away.

With her back to the creature, she sat down to let her nerves settle. She looked over her shoulder and admired her kill. The caterpillar was larger than she'd expected. The amount of meat she harvested would feed the entire village for days and she couldn't wait to bring it home. A loud crack thundered on the branch behind her, and she whipped her head around to see who approached.

"I should have known you'd follow me," she said with the slightest hint of irritation in her voice. "I said I wanted to be alone."

The nerve of him following me, she thought.

"I wanted to make sure you were all right." He walked to her and whistled as he neared the caterpillar. "Good grief, did you have to kill the largest behemoth on the tree? How many arrows did it take before it fell?" The yellow life fluid continued to leak out over the branch and he walked with light feet so he didn't slip on the wet surface.

"It took several," she said while beaming, "but now you're here and you can help me collect the meat."

His laughter filled the air as he pulled out his stone tools. "I would say well done, but I can see you're already proud enough." She playfully punched his arm. He massaged it to take out the sting and grinned. "Well, I guess we should get to work."

With the friendly banter aside, they cut into the flesh. They tried to get large swaths of the fur because it was useful material for winter coats. It took several trips to carry it all to the village where a portion of the meat would be salted and the rest would be smoked. It took the better part of the afternoon, but before long, they salvaged the valuable pieces of the creature. As she expected, the villagers welcomed the meat and they treated them both to dinner.

Her eyes wandered and she looked at Amridon several times, pleased the festive mood in the village overshadowed the potential Grimmox sighting. It was as though her eyes had a mind of their own and her stomach fluttered each time they rested on him. They had always been friends, but it never occurred to her there might be more. It seemed as though something was changing between them. After dinner, he had

The Final Offering

asked her to take a stroll, but she declined. She loved being with him true, but after the long day exhaustion overwhelmed her. After excusing herself, she made her way home hoping her refusal hadn't bothered him much.

***

Thula had always admired her parents because they were protective of the great tree. They had built their home inside a knot in the trunk that would otherwise have been useless, and thus preserved the symbiotic existence they nurtured over a generation. They had two levels with three bedrooms, and gentle holes carved out serving as windows to the outside world.

Trees and fire never got along, so the fairies had to be careful as to not risk a disaster. Most used warming pans in their bed to keep a comfortable temperature while they slept. The breeze coming through the window told Thula tonight would be cold. She grabbed her warming pan and walked back down to the main level, where she went to the clay oven and looked inside to find several coals still smoldering. Using a small shovel, she scooped a few into the pan and returned to her bed. Although she felt fearful she wouldn't sleep—her body still quaked from the news of the Grimmox sighing and her mind kept wandering toward the problem. It wasn't like her people to thirst for war like this and she didn't like it. Her eyes stared at the roof of her room and she thought she would never find sleep, but the hard work cleaning the caterpillar had drained her energy and she drifted off into the land of slumber.

The Final Offering

Chapter 2

The following day, Thula couldn't seem to get Amridon out of her mind. That evening as she was out for a stroll she ran into him. She invited him to join her and they ventured to the high-reaching branches. They walked side-by-side with her heart rate increasing as she stole a peek at his face in the silver light. In the soft darkness, she noticed his strong jaw, leading to the hard edges of his face and she realized how handsome he was. Over the past several days, she had sensed her feelings toward him changing as they matured, and hoped his were too, but neither had any idea how to approach this, choosing instead to avoid it altogether.

After the long walk, Thula sat on the edge of a bough with a clear view of the star-filled sky. The moon was full and loomed above. A slight breeze blew from the south and rocked the branch. She invited Amridon to join her.

A smile crossed her face as she looked up into his large brown eyes and tried to muster the courage to speak her feelings for once. "Thanks for your help yesterday. I never thought it would take so long."

Not ideal, she thought, *but at least it's a start.*

"It was my pleasure," he said as he returned her smile.

She shivered and welcomed his arms as he wrapped them around her. The heat felt good and her shivers diminished.

"Thula, there is something I must confess."

His eyes spoke to the seriousness of his tone and her body tensed in anticipation. *Could this be it?* She rested her arm on his shoulder as he continued.

"We've grown up together, and at times we treat one another like siblings, but for a while now my feelings have been different. I find you're on my mind more often, and when I'm not with you, I want nothing more than to be with you. There is something about you that draws me. I don't know what it means, and I don't know if you feel the same way, but I needed to get it out there. I hope to know how your thoughts too." His gaze slid down to his lap as he finished.

Goosebumps filled her flesh as excitement flooded her body. "Oh Amridon, I've been meaning to tell you I've had similar feelings." She turned and smiled, looking deep into his eyes. "No matter how hard I've tried to shrug them off, my mind always returns to you. I'm falling in love with you."

The words left her mouth and she couldn't believe how calm she sounded, at least in her own head. Inside, her body was a wreck. This was the day she had waited for and now that it was here, she didn't know how to continue.

Her mouth was still open as she intended to say more, but he cut her off and planted his lips on hers. His breath was fresh and warm, his tongue soft and delicate. He brought his hand up to her neck, grazing it before pulling her in closer.

The Final Offering

Breathing softly on her neck he whispered into her ear. "I love you too."

She eyed his soft lips with greed, voraciously yearning for more. He lay her down and kissed the nape of her neck before working down her body. His soft lips caused the tiny hairs on her skin to perk up like tiny needles. With each new kiss, her heart beat faster, wondering where his lips would explore next. She lost all conscious thought, and it appeared he had too. Her fingers curled and her nails dug into the rough bark of the tree. Fresh blood trickled into her mouth when she bit her lower lip in delight as he nibbled on her earlobe and his hot breath tickled her neck. The feeling overwhelmed her, and she wanted him to go further. This was what she had always wanted and couldn't believe it was happening. Nothing had ever felt better, she was close to losing herself and she wanted it to last forever.

She cracked open her eyes and looked up at the star-laden sky when she thought, *Wait, what are we doing?* Her mind worked to clear the haze of love.

While pushing him off, she said, "Stop, we can't do this." She hated the words as they escaped her mouth. As much as she wanted to move forward, it wouldn't be right. "We need to receive approval from our parents before we go any further."

He sighed and sat back. "Yes, but it doesn't make it any easier though." He stole a quick kiss before standing. "It seems right with you."

"Trust me, the last thing I wanted was to stop." She stood herself, now that her desires had come under rein, and her brain once again worked like normal. "It's getting late. Walk me back to my house, will you?"

He grabbed her arms and pulled her close. They walked side-by-side back to the tree trunk and descended until they reached her home. Not wanting to leave her this way, he leaned in closer, kissed her and whispered, "Good night."

Her lashes fluttered as her eyes rolled back into her head. It was never easy to stop, and she could succumb to the burning within her stomach if she wasn't careful, so she pushed him away again. "Good night, Amridon. I look forward to seeing you in the morning." She blushed and walked into her home, leaving him standing alone.

***

The following morning, Amridon showed up at Thula's doorstep. Her mother invited him in, and Thula rushed to his side. "What are you doing here?" she asked.

"I couldn't sleep last night," he whispered. "I can only think of you, and after our conversation, I needed to come here first thing in the morning to discuss our possible courtship with your parents."

She wanted to yell at him for rushing out like a love-struck fool, but something inside her agreed and she led him into her home.

Gorven's eyes grew wide. "Amridon! To what do we owe the pleasure of such an early visit?" he asked.

"If you have a moment, I would like to speak with you and Cellomes on something important." He looked at Thula and beamed. She had never wanted anything more

Gorven looked at Cellomes and shrugged. "We can spare a few minutes. I must attend a meeting this afternoon, but not until later." Gorven shifted in his seat as he leaned forward on the table. "So what important issue do you need to speak with us about?"

Amridon cleared his throat and looked at Thula. "You've both known me all my life. You are engaged in several business dealings with my family, and there has always been a closeness." Thula nodded, urging him to continue. "Your daughter and I have grown up together and I consider her to be one of my best, if not *the best* friend I have. As of late, our feelings have grown larger than that, and after several conversations, we realized we have each fallen for one another."

Gorven's eyes grew large, and he shifted in his chair as he listened before he urged Amridon to continue. Thula held her breath, praying her mother's sense of harmony would calm her father's rashness.

"We both recognize how young we are and we seek your blessing before we take our courtship any further. I want you to realize, I will do everything in my power to protect her. There is nothing and no one else I care more for than your daughter. I find I'm quite smitten and hope one day to be sealed with her, with your blessing, that is." Thula watched Amridon's eyes as he shifted his gaze back to her.

The words he uttered and the courtesy he offered was perfect. Thula couldn't have said it any better herself. If nothing else, he had won over her mother, but she expected more resistance from her father. There was a curse that came with being the youngest daughter, the baby, and he would want to hold on as long as possible. With eagerness, she shifted her attention to her father to listen to what he had to say in response.

Gorven looked at his wife with questioning eyes, unable to respond. Cellomes bought him time and voiced her opinion. "Amridon, I knew when you were both still toddler fairies, that one day this would come. I must say, you are quite the young man, and have a very promising future in front of you. I couldn't be any happier for you two."

Thula could tell her father hadn't expected his wife's response because he slumped back in his chair and shook his head. Thula rose and embraced her mother in a warm hug, pleased that her prayer had worked so far.

"Are the two of you mad?" her father said through strained lips. Thula knew he was struggling with the news, but hadn't expected such harsh words. "You're both too young. I will not allow my daughter to be promised in a courtship before either of you are free from the offering." He stood and pointed at Amridon. "If I'm correct, you're still eligible for one more," he spun on his heels and pointed at his daughter. "And you! I raised you better than this. You won't be free of this burden for two more years. What happens if you find yourself with child when you face this... this... annual tradition?" he asked. "What would happen to the child? For that matter, what would happen to you?" He paced behind his chair shaking his head as he continued his outbursts. "You're too young and I'll have no more of this conversation."

Thula ran forward pleading. "Father! It's not as though we're asking to be sealed now. That would come later when we are of age." A tear ran down her cheek from the corner of her left eye. "We both want to be together and realized this has been coming since we were children. We're seeking your permission to start a relationship now. I love him, father, and don't wish to give my heart to any other but him. Please, at least think about it!" Thula rested her hand on her father's arm.

Listen to reason, she thought. *You were young when you met my mother why should I be any different. You have to allow this. You want me to be happy, so stop standing in the way.* A million thoughts shot through her head, but somehow she couldn't vocalize any of them and stood like a little child afraid to speak the truth.

Gorven's face grew red with anger at his daughter's words. "This just proves how immature you are. Look at yourself!" he

The Final Offering

said with disgust filling his voice. "You're pleading and begging like a little child who doesn't get their way. Any person ready to pursue an adult relationship would handle this in a much better manner and would be respectful of their father's wishes and opinions on the matter. My answer remains no," he spoke with an air of finality. Amridon's mouth dropped open. He looked defeated.

Cellomes walked closer and grabbed her husband's arm, caressing his hand in her own. "Be reasonable, Gorven. They aren't any younger than we were when we found each other. And we did it behind our parents' backs." Her translucent wings fluttered, a sure sign of her increasing frustration. "The way they are acting is much more mature than we ourselves acted. They sought our blessing before making an impulsive decision. Your mind is still clouded by the governor's speech."

He turned and faced his wife. "I don't think it's wise. She is so young, and I am fearful of the offering. Look at her." He pointed to Thula. "I know many thoughts are filling her head, yet she stands there as quiet as a mouse."

"We decided long ago the odds of that happening were small. We only want her to be happy. If being with Amridon will give her that happiness. How can we deny it? We can't, just as we can't waste time worrying about the offering. If it happens, it happens, and is as Halothias, our God, has deemed his will."

She looked into his eyes. "How can we take away what may be her only chance at true love? What if she is selected? Would you be happy knowing our daughter is taken from us, never knowing the same love you and I both share?"

Her words seemed to work. A tear trickled down his face as he stared at his daughter. "I don't think the decision would be right. She is just a baby." This last just a strained whisper.

Cellomes pulled Gorven in closer. "Your baby has grown up." She chuckled. "It is time for you to face it and let go. Besides, is the decision not both of ours?"

He grinned. "The decision is ours." He let her go. "And I suppose you won't budge on your thoughts? You bless their relationship?" He waited as Cellomes nodded. "Then I guess you leave me little choice."

Amridon and Thula drew closer awaiting his verdict.

Gorven sighed. "I still think you are both far too young, but if it's your wish to develop a relationship who are we to stand in your way?" He threw his hands up into the air. "We bless your courtship."

Thula planted a soft kiss on Amridon's lips, before running to her parents. "Thank you, father." She hugged him before embracing her mother. She whispered into her ear. "And thank you, mother. I fear without your words of encouragement, we never would have received his blessing." Her voice wavered with jubilation.

Cellomes leaned in closer. "Sometimes he needs a reminder and a little encouragement to arrive at the correct decision. It is a skill you will learn and hone over the duration of your long relationship." She kissed Thula's forehead.

Thula grinned and thanked her parents again before grabbing her love's hand. They ran out of the house and into the warm spring air.

The Final Offering

Chapter 3

After their successful meeting with Thula's parents, they sought Amridon's to get their blessing too. Unlike Gorven, they were easy to convince and agreed without issue.

Now they no longer needed to hide their love, and they walked through the village hand-in-hand on most occasions. Today was no different as they strolled into the town commons, eager to learn of the governor's decision.

Thula had expected a quick response, but the council had convened for well over a week, much to her irritation, and that of the other members of the town.

It didn't help summer had arrived with a bang, and the heat had grown unbearable. It didn't make the crowd any calmer while awaiting the verdict. Sweat beaded on her forehead and trickled down the spine of her back as they joined the rest of the village.

Speculation and rumors were abundant during the past week and many had made their way to her ears. In her estimation, the fairies seemed divided on which course of action to take. She grew impatient as she waited in the breezeless summer heat for any word from their leader. Finally, the doors opened to the governor's residence, and two guards walked out. They stood at attention on the stairs and awaited his arrival. A hush fell over the crowd as they all looked on in anticipation.

The governor strode out of his quarters and stopped at the top of the stairs. His long gray hair sat in its customary ponytail, and his mustachios looked freshly waxed. The long week appeared to have taken a toll on him and he looked haggard, almost tired. He raised his hands to quiet those who still murmured.

"After a rather lengthy series of conversations, we reached a decision, and I have come to a conclusion." Thula's impatience grew as the anticipation built in the audience, all were eager to learn more. "We can't in good conscience march on the Grimmox just because someone may, or may not have spotted one of their kind within our branches." Anger erupted out of half of the villagers; the other half remained calm and tried their best to hide their relieved looks.

"Please, let me finish. We have found a solution amenable to both sides. As I was saying, we cannot attack them based on this information alone, but we cannot sit idly by and allow them to continue into our lands either. The council has agreed to reestablish the long-range sentry posts we abandoned many years ago. We will also create a unique force who we will train in espionage. If the Grimmox want to spy on us, we will return the favor. At the very least we'll find out if they're up to something."

The Final Offering

A compromise, he reached a compromise? How can it be possible? In her anger, she paced back and forth, stunned by the revelation and it appeared she wasn't alone. Nobody said much for several moments while they tried to digest the information. *How in the world can they think this is a good idea? There isn't enough cause to justify their actions.* Her mind shifted to Amridon who was a soldier. *How will I deal with him being gone on a mission? It will be lonely for sure, but what if something happens to him?* The wide-ranging thoughts continued to fill her mind.

The governor took advantage of the silence and continued. "All our lives, we have lived in fear of the Grimmox and their beastly ways. Every year we sacrifice one of our own to keep the peace. We have accepted this and we never falter in our allegiance to the treaty. We still don't want a war—and I don't see an end to the offering anytime soon—but if the Grimmox are planning an offensive, we'll be prepared."

Several of the older fairies spoke. "How will we man these outposts?"

"And what of the new force you mentioned?"

"All good questions and these are the reason it took us so long to reach an agreement. Our military strength is adequate to protect the town from an invasion, but we don't have the strength to man the new positions. We are temporarily putting a halt to our positioning by tattoo. That is, we are asking for volunteers to join the military and undertake the training necessary to take one of these new positions. If you're not willing to volunteer, you'll stay in your current job as dictated by your age of reckoning."

Thula's mouth dropped open in surprise. Her whole life she waited for her tattoos to become visible so she would know her position within the community. Everyone waited for that moment, and to hear of the halting of the process left her dumbfounded. She didn't know if she trusted the council. Something didn't seem right. They should have the best interests of the fairies in mind when making all their decisions. This felt underhanded as though the council had other ideas in mind. She needed to learn more and listened to what the other villagers had to say.

The governor's words brought voracious anger from many of the assembled villagers. "How can this be? Our tattoos determine who we are. It's how it has been since our founding days. How can *you* change all of that in one instant to fit your needs with the wave of a hand?"

A calm but authoritative voice called from the back. "Thank you, Governor Linotas, if you don't mind, I would like to speak." Thula turned her head and watched as an elder strode forward, pushing his way through the crowd. At first, it seemed he sent a wave of anger in his wake, but as the crowd recognized the cloaked figure, they parted and provided a path for him.

Where did he come from? Thula asked herself. She stood on her toes and noticed several other elders standing behind the gathering. In all the commotion, she hadn't noticed their approach and apparently, no one else had either. The elders never attended public forums, and most fairies were afraid of them; Thula was no different. She had learned at a young age—as did all Haloti—that the elders made all the decisions governing the Haloti. The governor was used as their voice and was nothing more than a figurehead.

The governor bowed to the elder. "Of course, Speaker Tremalo. By all means." He motioned for the elder to address the crowd.

The Final Offering

Tremalo removed his hood and showed his face. His head was bald, and he had smooth, dark skin that looked uncharacteristic given his presumed age, with a large ring in his nose and a bolt in his chin. His vivid tattoos climbed his neck and curved around the top of his head.

"Thank you. This may seem like a drastic measure, as though the council may be taking privileges with the Haloti by-laws, but please be assured, there are provisions that allow the governor to protect our way of life when threatened. Many of you may not view the situation as such, but the Grimmox are threatening us. They are a savage race who would like nothing more than the complete extinction of the Haloti."

What? Thula wondered. The Grimmox demanded the offering, this much was true, but she had never heard them referred to as savage or threatening. *Where are they getting this?*

"Most of you have never met a Grimmox, but I have, and their bloodlust knows no limits. They are warriors first and foremost, with little thought or care for Haloti life. They would kill one of their own to get what they want. If they are spying on us now, then we have to do something to show them we are not afraid. And we must do everything within our power to learn as much about them as we can. The time to act is now."

Thula watched as an old and wise villager stepped forward. "If I may, Elder?" Given the approval of Tremalo to speak, he turned and addressed the audience. "What the council is proposing goes against all we hold dear. If we walk down this path—changing our laws to suit and fit our needs—what's to stop the council from doing it again when the *council* deems it necessary? I'm not saying I'm against the plan, but I would like to know how we will restore our nation once these added measures are no longer needed.

"Also, you seem to know an awful lot about the Grimmox," he said in an accusatory voice. "If the Grimmox are as bloodthirsty as you state, why haven't they attacked us before now? It would seem we would be easy pickings, and your words are nothing more than a scare tactic." Thula joined the crowd as a hush fell over them. They weren't used to someone questioning the elders.

Tremalo wore a wide grin. "All good thoughts." He walked forward. "The simple answer is they need us. They've become used to our offering and rely on it. For what, we haven't discerned, but it seems it's vital to their way of life. This has been enough to hold them at bay for generations, but if they are venturing this far up the tree, then we can only presume an attack is imminent. We must take steps now to protect ourselves and gather information. Once the threat is neutralized, we will restore order and convert to the old ways."

Another villager stood and spoke her mind. Unlike the first speaker, she didn't wait for approval.

"I myself don't like it. We have laws for a reason and cannot change them whenever we deem it necessary, or when it fits our fancy. And your simple words here today are not enough to assure me you'll restore order. I'm afraid I will disagree with the decision, and I will do everything in my power to see it absolved." Raucous applause erupted from the crowd and she threw down her hands in disgust.

Tremalo motioned to several guards positioned near the rear. They made their way forward and grabbed the old fairy, carrying her off amidst her kicking and screaming—angry words dripping from her cracked, old lips. Thula watched as she disappeared down the stairs. Obviously going against the elders on this issue wouldn't be tolerated.

The Final Offering

Tremalo grinned as order returned to the crowd. If Thula didn't know any better, she would have assumed Tremalo had anticipated such an outburst, and in fact welcomed it.

"I must remind you all, of your place in our society. Our tattoos have determined our positions and we don't live in a democracy. We're using this forum to communicate with you how we intend to deal with this new threat. It isn't an opportunity to voice your displeasure or influence the opinions of the council. I beg you all to remember this." An eerie smile crossed his lips, and Thula couldn't tell why, but it made her shiver even in the Sun's warmth.

"Now then, on to the important matters. We're giving you the opportunity to improve your station, if only temporarily, by signing up for one of these two new positions." As the words left his mouth, several guards walked forward carrying wooden tables. A soldier sat down at each, with a paper and quill. It was obvious to Thula they expected many of the citizens to sign their lives away.

Amridon looked at Thula with excitement written on his face. She could tell he was eager to join and was utterly disgusted, wanting no part of it. "You are already in the service of the military. It was predetermined for you by your marks. What are you going to do?"

"I'm going to sign up for the espionage program. It sounds exciting and may give me the opportunity to get real combat with the Grimmox." He pulled away from her and joined one of the lines where many young Haloti already stood waiting.

Watching him walk away, her heart sank. It felt as though she was losing a part of herself. She hated everything the new program stood for. *My people are much more compassionate than this. Why are they so eager to join a program that that sounds like nothing more than the build-up toward war?* She wondered. To her dismay, she watched as the line grew ever longer. *I don't understand.* What they were about to do was dangerous, and she worried for Amridon. He was an adequate soldier, but she wanted to be there for him, to help him and have his back if a battle did break out.

Thula looked at the crowd, searching for her parents. She made eye contact with her father and groaned. He must have known what was going through her mind because he shook his head. A soldier wasn't something she ever envisioned for herself, she didn't know if it was in her. Then again, she could get information and understand the elders' true intents. Maybe this was what she was destined to do. *I don't know. Would I even make a good soldier?* On one hand, she wanted to follow the love of her life. On the other, she hated everything this new program stood for and she found it difficult to reconcile a decision with herself. With a large sigh, she broke eye contact with her father, running to join Amridon in line.

Gorven ran over and grabbed her arm. "Thula! What do you think you're doing?" he asked. "I thought you were against all of this."

She turned and looked up at her father with staunch eyes. "Well, this oaf," she pointed to Amridon, "is signing up for the espionage program. I can't let him go alone. He would probably get himself killed." She grabbed Amridon's arm. "Now that we have declared our love for one another, someone needs to watch his back and make sure nothing happens to him."

Gorven rolled his eyes. "I must say, I'm surprised, but we have always allowed you to make your own decisions. If this is what you wish, then so be it. Just promise me you'll be careful."

Cellomes joined them but remained silent.

"Oh father, I'm sure there is nothing for you to worry about, we'll just be spying. What did you make of…" She

The Final Offering

trailed off as she looked back over the crowd. The elders had disappeared. "Of the elder's speech?"

Gorven looked toward the governor's home, where Tremalo stood just moments ago. "I don't know, that's odd," he said. "I wonder where they went." He returned his attention to his daughter. "I can't say I like it. I mean, I wanted to act, but I never envisioned a situation where the council would take such drastic measures. Espionage? An increased military presence? These all sound like steps for a massive offensive, not just a retaliatory strike. I expected an eye for an eye, but this just seems like so much more." He lowered his voice. "And I agree with the old lady. There are no guarantees things will be restored. There is more to this than the elder indicated."

With a glance over her shoulder, she looked around to make sure no one had heard her father's words.

Returning to a normal volume he said, "I thought you disagreed with military measures and am a little surprised, that's all."

Thula leaned in closer and spoke in a hushed tone so only her parents could hear her. "I agree there was something suspicious in Tremalo's words. As we all saw though, there's no going against the council. The decision is made and there's nothing we can do about it." She shrugged and looked at Amridon. "He was eager to sign himself up and figured there was no better way to fight against these acts than to join them. At least I'll have inside knowledge as to what they plan. Maybe I can fight their actions from the inside."

Cellomes' face filled with sadness. "Just be careful. I can respect what you're doing, but one might call your acts treasonous. These are troubled times, and it wouldn't bode well for you or Amridon; I don't want them to catch you." She could tell her parents were proud of her, but their nervousness seemed too much.

"I'll be careful. I won't do anything to draw too much attention to myself. This is something I have to do. Even if it turns out to be nothing, at least I can be assured Amridon remains safe."

Her parents nodded in unison. Thula gave Cellomes a hug before her parents both departed and left the common area. Thula followed Amridon to the sign-up table when called forward. She signed her name and life away—at least for the time being—in service of the espionage regiment. Thula had an uncomfortable tightness in the pit of her stomach, and couldn't help but wonder if she made a bad decision. Her love for Amridon pushed her forward. She swore an oath before they whisked her away for the evening.

The Final Offering

Chapter 4

Two crows sat perched on an upper branch of the tree, bickering with one another in the warm summer heat. Thula sat above the birds with her two best friends, Alais and Myriani. It was Thula's last day before she began her training in espionage. More than anything, she wanted to take the time to reconnect with her friends and they settled on a stroll and a picnic. Thula leaned over the bough and told the birds to be quiet. They stared at her for several seconds before flying off in search of another perch.

"That's better. At least we can hear ourselves think now," she said while she tried to contain a giggle.

"We haven't spoken to you in weeks. Tell us more about how you and Amridon became a couple," Alais said. Alais was the shortest of the trio, with a slender and frail build. She had short hair, except for a braid she kept long and ringed around her head, almost like a crown.

Thula blushed and tried to hide her face. "We went for a stroll and it just came out we were in love with one another. What more do you want me to say?" She sighed in contentment.

Myriani leaned closer. She was the tallest and most muscular of the three. With long, flowing, brown hair that matched the complexion of her skin and a large bolt in her lip, she was quite the sight to behold. "But Amridon? I mean he's like our brother. He has followed us around like a lost puppy for as long as I can remember." Myriani was not one to mince her words.

"That's probably why we love each other so much. I can't picture a time when he wasn't there. My heart ached for his company," Thula said.

"You could've told us sooner. I thought we were friends." Myriani chastised her.

"Not that I haven't thought about it myself," Alais blushed. "He has grown up to be handsome. Just be glad you acted before I did." They all laughed at this, Alais being so shy and all.

They reminisced as they ate their lunch, remembering the lost days of their childhood, and the fun they had. Thula felt comforted and her heart warmed, there was nothing like the companionship of true friends to remind one of their blessings.

"Do you remember the time he fell in the water bucket?" Myriani asked, unable to hold back her laughter.

"How could I forget?" Thula said. "He was chasing us and forgot to use his wings when he jumped." The laughter overcame her and a moment passed before she continued. "He was soaked and so angry with us. I thought he would cry."

"What would he say if we asked him about it?" Alais asked.

The Final Offering

"He'd probably deny it ever happened. He wouldn't want to look weak. He's a strong young man, after all." They lost themselves in their laughter and Thula rubbed her side. A slight pain had developed after so much laughing.

After lunch, the talk turned. They were both eager to learn more about her new endeavor. "I still can't believe you start your training tomorrow. What made you do it? I mean, isn't it risky?" Alais asked.

Thula's look turned serious. "How much of the governor's declaration did you catch?"

"All of it. It all seemed frightening. Changes like this have never been made and I fear for our way of life," Myriani said. Her own glance turned outward to the nature they all cherished so much.

"I agree." Thula nodded. "The fact the elders joined the conversation has me nervous. Tremalo's words went a long way to bring many of the Haloti to his side, and I don't think I trust him." She shrugged trying to make sense of the reaction she had to one who was supposed to be so revered.

"Amridon was quick to sign up for the program and I felt the need, deep down in my stomach, to follow him. This way I can be by his side, but at the same time, figure out what the true intentions of these new programs are. There has to be more than what the council has revealed and I mean to get to the bottom of it," she said with determination.

Myriani pushed Thula's arm while laughing. "We all should've known better. You have always acted more like a man than you ever did a woman. Rushing out to join the spy program with the intention of revealing an evil plot, I mean, come on. Do you really fancy yourself some sort of heroine?"

"Shut up, Myriani!" She playfully pushed her away. "It's not like that. There's something else going on and I want to figure it out before it's too late. It's not as though I'm rushing out to accuse the elders. I couldn't bring them to justice all by myself, anyway." She smiled. "My hope is that I can uncover Tremalo's true intentions. If it's clear to me, I hope others in the program will be wise to it too. Assuming they aren't too blinded by their new positions that is."

Alais looked anxious. "Just be careful, would you? We like having you around, and we would hate for something to happen to you."

"And we don't want you spending the rest of your life in the military. Our parents are well off, and there is no way your tattoos would betray you by putting you in a position lower than your class. That hasn't happened in generations." Myriani pushed closer and whispered. "We have plans. Plans we laid out when we were children, remember? A life in service of the military would put an end to that. So don't go falling in love with the life of a spy."

"It's not as though the life of a military agent is lower class." Thula rebuked her friends. "While it might not be up to the standards we've been raised with, it's enough to live a happy life." A life in service of the military would be a harder life than she had planned for herself, but she didn't like how her friends criticized it. After all, Amridon had already started his career in the services. If they were sealed in life, it's what she would come to expect and she didn't understand why her friends had such a problem with it. "Besides, if I have a chance to put a stop to a wrong, shouldn't I? This could affect all of us."

"I guess you're right. It's just not something we ever envisioned." Alais, ever the peacekeeper, tried to backpedal from their earlier comments and patted Thula on the back. "We're happy for you. Instead of sitting on the sidelines, you're joining the fight. In a way, we envy you. I don't think either one

The Final Offering

of us," she pointed to Myriani and herself, "have the guts to do what you've done. If you believe Tremalo is up to something devious, then, by all means, do what you need to, and know you have our support." Myriani sighed but nodded in approval of Alais' words.

"Thank you, both of you. You have no idea how much that means to me." Thula looked to the sky. The sun had already begun its march toward the mountains on the western horizon where it would disappear in slumber until it crept back up in the east tomorrow. She was having fun with her friends but remembered she still had much to do before her training began.

"This was just what I needed. You have lifted my spirits like you always do, and I appreciate it."

"It was our pleasure," Alais said.

"And don't act like it's the end of our friendship. Your training will be hard, but you will still have free time to spend with us." Myriani said.

Thula smiled at both of them before standing. "I suppose you're right." She again looked to the sun. "It's getting late. I still have so much to do today, and I promised my family I would join them for dinner."

They agreed, and all began their climb down the tree. She hugged her friends one last time before retreating to her own home.

She walked inside, greeted by the warm scents of a caterpillar stew. It seemed her mother had pulled out all the stops. Underneath the first smells, she also caught the aroma of fresh bread. This was her favorite meal, but it was time-consuming. Her mother reserved it for special occasions.

She walked over and joined her mother, donning an apron. "Mother, you didn't have to do all of this. Alais and Myriani just reminded me that although I'm beginning my new journey tomorrow, I'll still be free to come home from time to time. It's not like you won't see me anymore."

Cellomes frowned at her daughter. "All of this? Is this not your favorite meal?" Thula nodded. "Why then, it's nothing at all." Her mother hugged her, and Thula saw a tear form at the corner of her mother's eye. "Come now, lend me a hand."

They worked for the rest of the afternoon making idle conversation while they finished preparing the meal. The stories brought back wonderful memories, and Thula felt homesick, even though she had yet to leave.

They finished plating the food when her father arrived home for the evening. Normally, her mother accompanied her father and worked in his office, but she had taken the day off to prepare this last family meal. Her two older sisters—Tilfin and Trana—who had moved out several years ago and now had lives of their own, even joined them. Gorven took his seat at the table, and Thula embraced each of her sisters, grateful for their presence. She had seen Trana the day before, but Tilfin had been busy as of late and it had been weeks since they had seen each other.

They offered a prayer to Halothias, founder of the Haloti before they began their dinner. "So tell me, are you excited for your new adventure? Or are you a little nervous?" Her father asked.

He caught her mid-bite, and she finished chewing before she replied. "Before today I would have said I was excited, but the closer it gets, the more nervous I become. My stomach has been in knots all day."

Trana, who had always been skeptical of the entire Haloti way of life, pursed her lips. She didn't trust the council, especially the elders who seemed to run it. She also didn't believe in the whole caste system they seemed to follow. Her

The Final Offering

intelligence motivated her, and she used it in her work as a teacher.

"I still can't believe you are going into espionage. It doesn't fit you," she said. "Then again, you've always been interested in adventure, so maybe it isn't too far off base."

Tilfin perked up at the conversation before Thula had a chance to reply. Thula wasn't the least bit surprised since her sister worked for the Church of Halothias as one of a number of priests, something only a few women accomplished.

"What is there to question? The elders have offered us a path, and the elders serve Halothias. We all serve Halothias, and what she is doing is admirable."

Here we go again. Her sisters were never in the same room together for long without breaking into an argument based on their differences in beliefs. She looked to Trana, expecting a rebuttal that would turn into a fight, but she surprised her. Rather than making a snarky remark of her own, she bit her lip and kept her comments to herself.

Gorven attempted to steer the conversation away from the argument so they could enjoy their last evening with Thula before she departed, and it worked well enough for them to celebrate their sumptuous dinner, and bask in their time together.

Tilfin was quick to dismiss herself after they ate, stating she had to rise before sunup for an early service. Gorven breathed a sigh of relief when she left, and Trana didn't waste any time offering her true thoughts.

"Why are you *really* joining the program? I've been told you're doing it to be with Amridon, but I don't believe it. You've always been independent."

Thula pondered her sister's words long and hard. She didn't know how much she wanted to relay of her true intentions. The last thing she wanted was to endanger her family in any way because she had treasonous questions. Her father nodded, and she proceeded. "That part is true. I love Amridon with all of my heart and wish to make sure he survives whatever he might get himself into; you know how he is."

"Love? What do you know about love?" Trana asked. "You're too young and have experienced too little in your short life to know what true love is."

"Love doesn't have a time frame. Don't let your own insecurities—and the fact you're still not in love yourself—cloud your judgment. I wake up and my heart aches for him. I go to bed, and I want to be nestled in his arms. Just the idea of being near him brings a smile to my face. If that isn't love, then I don't know what is." She was angry with her sister.

Why is she so quick to condemn my feelings? She asked herself, even though she figured it to be jealousy. Nothing else made any sense.

"Besides, what does it matter to you?"

Trana offered a grin. "I don't care about that. It's your life. If you think you're in love, then so be it, but it isn't enough of a reason to run out in service of the council. You're better than that. As your big sister, it's my job to be sure you don't ruin your life."

Thula sighed, rolling her eyes. "Yes, well, thank you for your vote of confidence I'm glad you will let me live my life," she said. "As I said before, my love for Amridon is only part of it. I don't like what the council is doing, and the elders have something else in mind. I figured what better way to unravel, or uncover their plot than to be a part of it. Work it from the inside, you know?" She looked up at the ceiling. Her reservations came back to the surface, and she was unsure she could go through

The Final Offering

with it. But what choice did she have now? The training started tomorrow. There was no backing out now.

"Now that I can admire." Trana nodded. She looked around the home and lowered her voice. Although they were inside, you could never be sure if someone was listening. "I have heard things; things that don't quite add up. I too think the elders have ulterior motives."

"That's it. Listening to the words dripping from Tremalo's mouth sent a shiver up my spine. They are using this whole thing as a cover-up for the start of an invasion. Now, I'm wondering if a Grimmox was even spotted." Thula paused while she considered her words. She didn't want to seem insolent—they were taught their entire lives to respect the decrees of the Elders—but wasn't that the exact problem? "It was all nothing more than a giant setup used to manipulate the council, and gain support from the villagers, to change our laws and increase our military force, by creating a means for gathering information."

Trana smiled, but Gorven and Cellomes looked much more uncomfortable as they shifted in their seats. Thula wanted to discuss more with her sister, but Gorven rose to his feet.

"That's enough, girls." He glanced at their windows before proceeding in a hushed tone. "What you both speak of is treason. I can't say I disagree with you, but we need to be careful how we talk about it. There are always people listening. We should put an end to this and turn in for the evening." He turned to Thula. "Your training will require much from you. You need your rest; tomorrow will be a busy day."

Thula knew her father spoke the truth. They all chipped in to clear the table and clean up the dishes. Her parents excused themselves for the evening and Thula walked her sister to the door. She gave her a hug and Trana spoke in a whisper.

"Although I admire what you're doing, it will be dangerous. Please be careful."

"I will, Trana. Just as I'm looking out for Amridon, he'll be there to keep me safe too."

Her sister turned to leave, offering a look of sorrow as if they would never see each other again. She turned and pulled Thula close once more.

"There is something else I should mention. I have joined an underground resistance group. The elders need to be deposed, and we mean to act when the time is right. Much of what we've heard aligns with your fears. I will pass any information I gather along to you. I ask that if you find anything out, you do the same."

Now it all made sense to Thula. The anger and resentment, what she picked up on as jealousy wasn't directed at her, but instead the council and the elders. "I will and thank you. You be careful too." Trana smiled at her little sister's concern.

Trana departed, and Thula closed the door, before retiring to her room. She climbed into her bed, eager to drift off to sleep, but the information Trana had shared left her unsure as she tossed and turned all night long.

The Final Offering

Chapter 5

Thula awoke well before the sun crested the eastern horizon. A biting breeze blew in through her bedroom window and raised the tiny hairs on her skin. She wasn't rested at all since she had only slept for a few hours because she couldn't shut off her mind. With the day still in front of her, she started her preparations.

She packed her bags and only needed to gather a few last-minute items. She cleaned her teeth and face before heading down to the kitchen for breakfast. To her surprise, Cellomes was already hard at work preparing the meal.

"Good morning, Thula. I gather you didn't sleep well last night?" She waited as her daughter nodded before offering a consolatory smile. "I didn't either. I worry too much about you, but it's not my place. It's your choice, and I will honor that." She paused as Thula sniffed the air, taking in the aromas of the cooking food. "Please have a seat. I have prepared fresh oatmeal with spiced apples, and hot tea."

Thula's stomach grumbled at the description, and she pulled a stool up to the table. "Thanks. I can't say there haven't been times where I thought I was crazy, but there is nothing I can do about it now." She watched as her mother set a plate and a steaming clay mug of tea before her. "You didn't have to go to all of this trouble for me. I was planning on a piece of toast."

Cellomes frowned. "You didn't think I would send you out the door without a proper breakfast, did you? Halothias only knows what slop they'll be serving you during your training. It's my duty to see you off with a proper meal in your stomach."

"Well, I very much appreciate it." She grinned as she dug into the bowl of oatmeal and apples.

Cellomes pulled up a stool of her own and sat down opposite her daughter with a plate of food. "What you're doing is brave. I would never have the guts to do it." She paused while she took a sip of her tea and gazed over the cup. "Just promise me you will be careful. I don't want anything to happen to you." Unshed tears shimmered in her eyes.

"Thanks, mom." She walked over and gave her a hug. She grew tired of hearing from everyone she needed to be careful, but she couldn't say she blamed them either. At least she knew many people loved and cared about what happened to her.

"I promise I won't do anything crazy... I'll leave that to Amridon." She couldn't help herself and smirked. "Everything will be all right. Besides, I'll be in training for several months, and I'm sure most of this will blow over by then," she said, even though deep down in her stomach she wasn't sure.

The early morning rays of sunlight cast a bright hue through the main level of their home in the tree. They finished their breakfast as her father joined them. He offered his pleasantries

The Final Offering

before Thula gathered her bags and departed her home, saying a tearful goodbye to both parents. She climbed the twisting staircase wrapped around the trunk that would take her to a higher level, and to her destiny.

***

After arriving at a higher branch, a soldier informed her the barracks were in a large cavity carved into the trunk. The soldiers had split the barracks in two, women occupying one side, and the men the other. An officer sat at a table outside the entrance. Thula checked in and received her bunk assignment. The other girls worked around her to carve out their own personal space within each assigned area. She did her best to make her bunk comfortable and homey, seeing as how it would serve as her home for the next couple of months. The quarters were plain and drab, and she thought it smelled musty, which irritated her nostrils. She unpacked her bags and dressed in her uniform, which she found stuffy and unflattering, but she had to get used to it.

She donned her hat when a blast from a whistle filled the morning air. The new soldiers looked around at one another, unsure of what they should do. *Here goes nothing,* she said to herself after realizing she was no longer in charge of what she could and could not do. They filed out of their quarters and onto the main tree branch. It was large and flat, serving as the perfect training grounds. Three officers stood in a row several hundred paces down the branch. They yelled and issued commands in gruff voices—gruff presumably from the many years of yelling at recruits—just as they were doing on this morning.

The recruits followed several of the other well-seasoned soldiers who had signed up for the new program and lined up for the officer's review. Thula recognized several of her friends, many of whom it surprised her to see. Her eyes fell on Amridon standing in the front row and her heart fluttered. *Why does he have to look so handsome?*

"Listen up, many of you have already gone through our basic training program, so this may be redundant, but we will put you through it again as a few of our tactics have changed. Since this is a new program, we also wanted to group you all—new and old—to build cohesion within the unit. As a result, any rank you may have held before will drop to match the rest of the new recruits." He took several steps forward. "You are all recruits from here on out." He turned his head and looked at another soldier. "Sergeant, they're all yours."

The soldier grinned. "Thank you, Captain." He turned and paced before the new recruits. "For the next two months, you will do exactly as I command. When I give you an order the only acceptable response is, 'Yes sir!' Do I make myself clear?" A boisterous and unified, "Yes sir" met his words, and the sergeant smiled from ear-to-ear. There was nothing like a new group of recruits eager to prove themselves.

"Very good. You're in for several difficult weeks of training, which will begin with getting in shape. We'll keep it nice and simple today, starting with a run." He laid out the course which would take them off the maple tree and onto the neighboring aspen.

Gazing around the gathered soldiers, Thula counted thirty-two recruits. They formed a single line and followed the sergeant while another seasoned soldier brought up the rear to make sure everyone kept up the pace.

They ran down the branch and neared the end when Thula saw the sergeant jump in the air. His translucent wings fluttered as he floated and landed on a branch of the aspen. He stopped and turned to watch the recruits try the jump.

The Final Offering

The first one wore a confident smirk on his face. He ran full speed and flapped his wings, misjudging the distance. He was short and missed the branch; panic filled his face as he flailed his arms. His forward momentum carried him. Though he rolled and twisted, before coming to a stop on his back with a bright red, embarrassed face.

Amridon was next in line. Seeing the failure of the first runner, he seemed to make sure he used his wings to his advantage; they moved in a flurry and almost became invisible. He landed a few paces from the sergeant.

Thula had been near the end of the line and it was now her turn. Only one other recruit mistimed their jump, and she wasn't about to be the third. She had been hunting and running through the trees all of her life and should be just fine. Still, she talked herself into completing the jump and visualized it in her head. Each step became easier as she bounded down the hard, gray wood of the tree branch, light on her feet, and jumped. Her wings fluttered, ever so slightly, as she flew and landed. The wings certainly wouldn't have allowed her to fly, but they did offset a part of her weight making her as graceful as a butterfly as she flew. Back on the tree branch, she slowed her momentum and came to a stop, grinning from ear-to-ear as she caught the stares from several of the recruits. Without another word or an order, she walked to her spot in line.

They spent the rest of the day running through many exercises. The first steps were always to make sure everyone was in shape, and judging by the first day, they would be the most well-conditioned troops the Haloti ever had in training. Thula just hoped her body became used to the rigorous activity sooner, rather than later. Her body ached—muscles she didn't even know existed before today hurt—and she wanted to crawl into bed. *What have I got myself in to?* She wondered. It was still early when she returned to her quarters, and her stomach growled, reminding her of how hungry she was.

She stripped off her training clothes and put on a fresh shirt before heading down to the hall that served as a cafeteria. Most of the recruits already filled it, and she grabbed a tray while standing in line. She surveyed the room as she waited. Amridon and several of his friends sat at a table on the outskirts. His eyes lit up when they locked with hers and he waved her over to him.

He smiled as she sat. His lustful gaze wasn't lost on her as he allowed his eyes to linger up and down her body. She blushed.

One of the other recruits said, "Thula, that was a fantastic first jump. How did you pull it off in such a graceful manner? Many of us used our wings too much, to our own detriment." Amridon's friend poked another next to him in jest.

Thula blushed again and was about to speak, but Amridon answered for her. "She's been hunting our lands since she was a young girl." He grinned as he continued. "Listen to me when I say, she's agiler than any recruit here."

She thanked him with her eyes, then lowered them and ate her dinner. The food tasted bland on her tongue, but it satisfied her churning stomach. Amridon and his friends continued their conversation, and she listened in, just happy to rest many of her sore muscles.

"I'm just glad the council finally did something about them. I mean, the nerve..." one of them said.

Amridon nodded. "I can't wait for one of the pale creature's evil eyes to come into my crosshairs. I'll have no problem putting an end to their miserable existence." He laughed while his friends urged him on further.

Thula rolled her eyes. "What if they have a family? Have you thought of the repercussions?" She looked at each of them.

The Final Offering

"You're all so angry, and I can't for the life of me fathom why." She snorted.

What do boys know about killing, anyway? And yet they are all so eager.

Amridon looked flummoxed. "I'm just thinking about those who are most dear to me. The Grimmox threaten our existence. It's as though I've waited my whole life for this opportunity. I apologize if I seem eager." He moved closer to her and tried to bring her into a hug. "I'm just trying to protect you." He winked at one of his friends across the table.

She brushed him off and stood. "I've already proven I can take care of myself." She looked at her plate of food and picked up what remained. "I've lost my appetite." She turned, threw what remained of her food in the trash, and stormed out of the hall.

As she left, she could hear Amridon. "Guess I pushed her over the edge. I will pay for that later."

The Final Offering

Chapter 6

Thula returned to the barracks miffed by the conversation with Amridon and plopped herself down on the bed. She noticed the lack of thickness in the mattress when she jarred her backside. It would be a difficult night of sleep, but what night hadn't been difficult lately? Her face flushed, and she tried to calm the emotions flowing through her body. She found it difficult though, as it was hard to watch someone you love transform so much right before your eyes. Or had he always been this way, and she hadn't noticed? He had always been a calm man, and she didn't like this sudden change in aggressiveness. Never in her wildest dreams had she seen him act this way, and it didn't seem right to her. Then again, she had always been much more of a forgiving person.

Although it was still early—the sun hadn't even disappeared over the horizon yet—she climbed beneath the covers, pulling them up tight to her head, and closed her eyes. She didn't think sleep would come, but couldn't think of anything else to do in her current state. Fortunately, the rigorous hours of exercise earlier in the day had left her body fatigued. The lack of food—since she had thrown the bulk of it in the trash—aided the exhaustion overwhelming her body, and she soon drifted off to sleep.

The worries of the evening drifted away, and she slept so soundly that she didn't even wake up when others made their way to the barracks. Given everything on her mind, she was thankful the sleep was dreamless—at least as far as she remembered.

Thula awoke the following morning refreshed, but with an aching stomach. She opened her eyes and basked in the warmth offered by the morning sun. While yawning and stretching her arms, she urged the aftereffects of a long night of sleep to leave her body and climbed out of bed. While putting on a fresh set of clothes, the events of the previous night came flooding back to her. She had greeted the morning calm and relaxed, but her uneasy feelings and anger crept back to the forefront of her mind. *What am I going to do with Amridon? He isn't acting like himself.*

Shaking her head to clear it, she cleaned up and changed her clothes before grabbing a bite to eat. The dining hall was deserted, and she thought it fortunate most people were still asleep, leaving her alone with her thoughts. With her stomach full, she walked outside and climbed up several branches. The rough texture of the branch felt comforting on her feet. A thin layer of dew covered the branch and tickled her toes as the sun's

The Final Offering

rays kissed her exposed skin. At the end of the branch, she looked around and smiled. She had a few hours before her daily training began and she wanted to stay away from Amridon until she sorted everything out.

Taking a seat, she dangled her feet over the edge of the branch and stared at the vast expanse of nature stretched out before her. Birds tweeted and fluttered through the sky. A squirrel on a neighboring tree bounded from bough to bough. She looked at the ground and noticed their most recent crops sprouting, showing the first signs of their green tentacles poking through the lush, black dirt. To the west, she saw movement at the mines.

The warming, yet still crisp morning air cleared her mind, and she lost herself in her thoughts when she heard someone approaching. She was high enough up, and it was early enough in the morning, that no one else should be about, which meant it could only be one person. She sighed and turned to face the newcomer.

"I came up here to be alone, Amridon. I would ask you to take your leave."

He smirked. "Come now. You can't still be upset about last night. Talk to me," he pleaded.

Anger came bubbling to the surface and filled her eyes. "Talk to you? What would I possibly have to say to you? she asked.

"You know how it is." He shrugged. "I guess I have to play it up for my friends. It's what we do."

"Not at my expense, you don't." She turned and gazed out over the horizon. "You know full well I can take care of myself and I don't need someone watching over me. You're making me appear weak in front of the other recruits."

"Come on, they understood it was in good fun. They've seen you in action. You can't think they listened to a word I said."

"It doesn't matter. We've confessed our love for one another. What gives you the right to make fun of me, even if it's only in jest? It hurts just the same."

He moved in closer to her, to offer comfort, but she pulled away. "Thula, I'm sorry, okay? I'll be more careful."

She spun on her heels and looked into his eyes. "You're missing the point. Your attempt at humor at my expense was only part of why I was upset. The way you've been talking isn't like you, and it has me worried. Why do you harbor so much resentment toward the Grimmox?" She stared hard at him.

Clarity dawned in his eyes. "I don't understand why you don't hold more?" He shot back. "You've grown up hearing all the same stories. We've suffered persecution for too long, confined to the upper echelons of our tree. We have to go out of our way to make it to the ground, and don't get me started on the offering." His anger increased, the veins in his neck popping out with each punctuated statement. "It's time we changed many things."

She rushed to his side and put her hand on his back. "But that's just it. We're basing all of our decisions right now on tales handed down from generation to generation. I don't know what happened. Neither of us was there. How can we start a war with them when none of us have ever even seen one in the flesh?"

"Does it matter if we've never seen one before? We don't have the freedom we deserve, and they take one of our young every year. For what?" His eyes drifted to the ground. "It's hard not to believe when you hear the countless retellings. I need to do something." He stood rigid, looking ready to fight right then and there.

The Final Offering

"As you've said on many occasions, I've heard all the same stories and you don't see me rushing out thirsting for blood. I'm giving the Grimmox the benefit of the doubt like my parents *taught* me, and I would expect more of our generation to do the same." She sniffed in derision. "I mean, aren't you sick of just following everything that's shoved down our throats with no evidence of support in the least?"

Amridon looked deep into her eyes. "Then tell me. Why did you join the spy program? It seems counter-intuitive to what you're saying."

She leaned in closer to him. "There are two reasons. First, I wanted to be with you. I could tell you were joining the program no matter what, and if I wanted to ensure your safety, I needed to follow you." She offered him a smile. "Besides, I love you and couldn't stand being without you."

He smiled. "What is the other reason?" he asked.

"I don't trust the elders." He didn't like her words. She saw it in the way his eyes narrowed, and she turned away from him before continuing. "I will take part in the program, and will follow my assigned duties. If I see a Grimmox behaving in a manner that in any way endangers the Haloti, I will do what is necessary to protect our people." She turned and faced him. "But, if this is an act by the elders, I will do whatever is needed to show our people the truth."

He brought his hand up and tried to quiet her. "You shouldn't speak of such things out in the open."

"I honestly don't care, Amridon. What they've asked of us isn't fair, especially if it isn't the truth. Don't you see that?"

He brushed a strand of hair away from her eyes. "I care too much for you to lose you because you went against the council. You need to be careful. Don't you remember how they escorted the old woman out during the governor's speech?" He sighed and leaned in as she looked up into his eyes. "Can we put this behind us?"

"Yes." She smiled. "Now that I've explained my position, I ask you to keep your comments to yourself. I'm going to sort this out." She knew he didn't agree with her stance, but she let him off the hook.

"Of course, my love." He leaned in for a kiss.

He tasted of fresh mint. As he pulled back, an emptiness filled the pit of her stomach. She didn't want it to stop, but they had other things to attend to before training. "You must be starving. Let's grab you some breakfast. Judging by yesterday's activities, we will need all our energy today."

"Nothing has ever sounded better." He hooked his arm through hers and smiled. They made their way down through the branches and entered the dining hall.

The Final Offering

Chapter 7

Over the next several weeks, their basic training progressed. The sergeant had them running all day every day, and each recruit gained the skills necessary to jump from branch to branch. There was never a fall or a mistimed jump. Thula had never felt more alive, or in better shape. Many of her reservations about the elders had passed. There had been no more sightings of the Grimmox, and life seemed as if nothing had ever happened. If anything, she now had a job and a purpose and life was good.

Their basic training was nearing its end, and soon they would all graduate to their more- advanced work. The officers were kind enough to grant an extended week of leave to go home and visit with their families before embarking on their next part of training. The sergeant informed them they would have little free time once the espionage training began, and he urged them to enjoy life away for as long as they could. She looked forward to a little rest and relaxation, and of course private time with Amridon. Very few opportunities to be alone had materialized during the training and she missed him, even though she saw him daily, it wasn't the same.

On the morning of their last day of training, she didn't notice anything different. It seemed like any other day. She stood at attention for roll call, with Amridon to her left, and waited in anticipation for their orders. They stood in their rows as the sergeant approached. Eager to hear what they had in store for the day, she was shocked when he stood there and stared at them.

After several moments of standing in line, waiting for the inevitable, the captain made his approach. Ever a fan of the dramatic, it would seem he enjoyed stretching the moment out. He eyed the fine line of recruits and smiled broadly. Obviously pleased by the discipline and dedication they displayed, he stared at the rows spread out across the tree and spoke to the sergeant in private, before stepping toward the front.

"Ladies and gentlemen, I would like to be the first to congratulate you on a job well done thus far. I spoke to the sergeant and given all you have put forth we would like to skip the remaining training we had in store for you today." Grins appeared on many of the recruits' faces, including Thula, as the captain continued.

"I thought you might like that. Instead, we will have one final, short run, and you will graduate. I implore you to enjoy your week of freedom. When you return, the intensity will increase." An eager smile appeared on his face, reminiscent of the longing eyes of a young child with a piece of candy

The Final Offering

displayed in front of their eyes. He looked toward the sergeant. "You may begin."

The sergeant stepped forward and saluted the captain as he left. "You all heard the man. Just a simple run and you'll be dismissed." His eyes showed a twinkle of mischief in them that didn't bode well for the new graduates. "Follow me," he said as he jogged down the branch, and the recruits followed.

The sun was bright that morning, and the air was thick with humidity. It wasn't long before beads of sweat dripped down their already red and hot faces. Thula was in fantastic shape, and the run didn't bother her yet, but their climate was dry and she was unaccustomed to the humid air. A week of rain had plagued their neck of the woods and Thula only hoped the heat of the morning was a sign they were in for a dry spell.

She took her time and fell in line behind Amridon, watching as his muscles flexed and contracted with each move he made. If nothing else, it helped to pass the time. They passed the middle trunk of the aspen tree to the south, and she spotted five little heads of baby birds peeping over the edge of a nest high in the tree. Their mother sat perched on a branch above, angrily chirping at the fairies as they ran passed. She was always amazed by the innate motherly instincts of creatures in nature. It was a sight to behold.

A sudden change in course by the sergeant pulled her out of the state of her wandering eyes and back to the path in front of them. They leaped from the bough of the maple and landed on a lower branch of the aspen. So far, they had stuck to a specific course, but this was something new. They appeared to be making their way down the aspen. Confirming her suspicions, they made their way to the ground. He turned toward the south, and they followed. It became clear they were heading toward a much larger, and older, cedar tree.

They had stayed well away from this large behemoth on all of their earlier runs because the tree was home to several squirrels, and an owl and hawk who liked to perch on the upper branches—never at the same time, of course—as they stalked a meal in the valley stretching below to the east. Her nerves ran taut as her stomach tied itself into knots with the unexpected route. *What is happening? Why have we changed routes?* She wondered as she tried to gauge the other trainee's reactions. *There are too many predators and I don't like it.*

The journey up the cedar was difficult; there were no paths or already well-trod trails, which made the climb treacherous. She did her best, even as her muscles screamed in agony from the new and different exertion.

They faced little resistance—other than the chattering of an angry squirrel who seemed displeased by the interruption—and reached the top of the new tree. Out of breath, they stopped for only a moment to take in the view and drank from their canteens before heading back. By the time they made it to the ground, they were exhausted and their stomachs screamed in pain. Lunchtime had already passed, and none of them had prepared for an endurance run. She had gained a slight pain in her side that became far more than just a nuisance.

Amridon slowed so she could catch him. "Are you alright? You look a little pale."

She tried to smile, but her lips curled as a shock of pain traveled up her side. "I'm fine. Just a cramp."

The Final Offering

His eyes showed his general concern as they shifted to her side. "Can you finish? We still have an hour at least. I should've warned you they tend to engage in a long run on the last day. It's kind of a rite of passage."

She rolled her eyes. *Of course, he knew,* she thought.

"Yeah, a little heads up would've been nice." She sighed knowing that his time estimate was right. "I'll be fine. Most cramps pass quickly. I'll just have to continue on and push through the pain."

He nodded before turning and regaining his position just in front of her.

The one-hour timeframe Amridon had quoted wasn't right. The sergeant took them to the top of the aspen before allowing them to jump to the maple that was their home. As they neared dinnertime, they arrived back at their branch. The captain stood there, with several other officers, and waited for them to file into their ranks. Several of the recruits looked like they wanted to vomit, but regained their composure and stood straight.

"I expected a short run, but I'm sure the sergeant had a couple detours for you." The captain looked at the sergeant and laughed. "Either way, I'm proud of you all. From this day forward, you are no longer recruits. Each of you has earned an increase in rank." He waited for a beat before he continued. "There is a couple of you who have shown exemplary skills throughout the training, and I would like you to come forward when I call your name. Ploura, Amridon, and Thula, please join me."

Ploura and Amridon walked forward without hesitation. Thula, on the other hand, was shocked. She had never expected recognition for anything and the butterflies returned to her stomach. Realizing she was taking too much time, she stepped forward and joined the other two.

With the three soldiers in line, the captain addressed the assembled crowd. "From this day forward, anyone in service before signing up for this program will return to their former ranks as we move into the next phase of your training. Anyone new to the service when they volunteered will from this day forward be a private. Congratulations on your accomplishments." He clapped his hands as many eager smiles filled the faces of the young recruits. This was the day they had been waiting for and now they all relaxed.

"Ploura and Amridon were both corporals before the program." He continued, once the applause quieted. "I am happy to say that from this day forward they have both been promoted to the rank of sergeant, and I expect them to be treated with the respect befitting their position, is that understood?"

The soldiers shouted with a resounding, "Yes, sir."

The captain dismissed Ploura but told Amridon to stay up front. He turned to Thula. "I am happy to announce Thula has surprised many of us. Her athletic abilities, endurance, and overall scores were higher than any other recruit. I'm also pleased to announce, from this day forward, Thula will carry the rank of corporal and is due all the respect befitting the position."

Thula wore a surprised look on her face. Not knowing what else to do, she saluted the captain. He returned it with a broad smile as he excused her and waited as she walked back to her place in line.

The Final Offering

The captain turned and looked at Amridon, before addressing the rest of the soldiers. "Now, on to our last bit of business. Amridon, you have proven your skills worthy through your second bout of basic training, and have helped the new recruits in a manner that is admirable. As such, we are naming you unit commander. You will answer to me, but everyone else standing out here today will answer to you, is that understood?" Thula watched as pride flooded her love's face. An overwhelming sense of satisfaction filled her as she listened to the praise heaped upon him.

The captain dismissed them and ease settled over all the soldiers as they relaxed. Several of them rushed over and congratulated Amridon. He thanked them and fought his way to Thula.

She smiled as he embraced her in a hug. "Congratulations, sergeant," she whispered into his ear. "I have to say, it's special to be in the arms of someone so accomplished."

"Thanks, but I'm the one who should feel special. I've never heard of a promotion from a recruit to corporal after finishing basic. It's a huge honor."

She didn't know what to say and cast her eyes down, a slight flush blooming through her cheeks at the accolades. "I was caught off guard, to say the least." She looked at the other soldiers who drifted toward their quarters. "What do you say we get packed up and head home?"

He kissed her cheek. "I would have to say nothing has ever sounded better."

They gathered and packed their belongings before meeting. Their military garb was gone, replaced by the silk clothing they were accustomed to wearing. He wrapped his arm around her waist and they set off for their home, the sun setting behind the mountains to the west.

The Final Offering

Chapter 8

Darkness settled above Thula and Amridon. The twinkling of the stars filled the sky as they walked down the tree hand-in-hand. The soft flashing of yellow lights surrounded the pair, the fireflies dotting the night air. Crickets chirped filling the empty space of night as the moon made its appearance.

Although Thula enjoyed the alone time with Amridon and wanted to soak him up, she was excited to see her parents too. The months away had been hard on her and she yearned for their companionship. They neared her home when Amridon stopped her.

"As much as it pains me to do so, I should leave you here. I don't want to interfere with your reunion," he said.

Although he had a point, she couldn't help it and frowned. "I wish you would come in for a minute, but it's for the best."

She leaned in for a kiss but stopped short. "I've been with you every day for the past two months, but it seems like I've barely seen you. Promise me we'll get to spend some alone time together during this break."

"You're my top priority." He grinned. "Tell your parents hello for me."

She nodded as he leaned in closer. They were both hot and sweaty after the afternoon's run, so she didn't want to make them both uncomfortable by pressing too close. Amridon rested his lips up against hers and they exchanged a short, but delightful kiss. She wanted it to last longer but didn't want to keep him, as she was sure his parents were expecting him too. The last thing she wanted was to make them worry, so she took a step back.

"Good night, Thula. See you in the morning."

Lost in the moment of the kiss, her eyelashes fluttered. "Good night to you too, Amridon. I'll be patiently awaiting your presence." She smiled and watched him walk away. Something deep down seemed to ache when he left, but she brushed it aside and turned back toward her home.

She walked through the door and found her parents deep in conversation. They turned their heads at her arrival and the joy of her homecoming was prevalent on their faces as they rushed to embrace her.

Gorven beamed at her. "Thula, my dear, how blessed we are to have you home."

"My angel, how lovely to see your beautiful face," Cellomes said as she hugged her. "The house has been so empty

The Final Offering

since you've been away." She looked at her daughter. "Where's Amridon? I assumed he would've accompanied you home." A moment of fear flashed through her eyes. "Nothing happened to him I hope."

Thula laughed. "No, no. He's fine. We split right before we arrived here. He didn't want to take away from our time together. We'll see enough of each other over the next week, but he sends his regards."

"How sweet of him." She offered a warm smile. "You must be famished. Come in and sit. I will fix you a plate while you tell us everything."

Thula rubbed her stomach. "That sounds terrific. Come to think of it, I haven't eaten since this morning."

Cellomes grabbed a clay bowl and ladled stew into it while Thula recapped everything that had happened since she last was home. At several points, both of their eyes grew wide as they listened with bated breath, taking in all she experienced and accomplished.

Gorven waited for her to finish before he said, "Amridon is right. You should be proud. I've never heard of anyone coming out of training as a corporal."

"Your father and I couldn't be any happier for you. We knew you would be successful." She beamed with pride at Thula.

"Yes, yes, very much so," her father said. "Tell me what else. Have you learned anything? I mean you were nervous going into the program, and you mentioned you wanted to find out if the council was up to anything. I'm eager to hear what you've uncovered." He said with eagerness filling his voice.

"There's nothing to report, father." Her shoulders slumped as she shrugged. "So far, I haven't seen anything out of the ordinary. In fact, I haven't even seen a member of the council. I have to imagine it's what one would expect of a basic training program." She grabbed the loaf of bread sitting in the middle of the table and tore off a large chunk. "I can tell you they've worked us to the bone. I don't think I've ever been in better shape." She flexed her muscles. "Just this morning, we went on our final run—which included a trip up the cedar tree—that kept us moving for half the day."

Gorven whistled. "That would explain your appetite then." He chuckled. "So what's next, if I may ask?"

She finished the piece of bread in her mouth. "Well, we have a week off, and when we return, we will begin our espionage program preparation." Her father nodded in understanding. "From what I hear, it will be a mixture of class work and hands-on training. I'll tell you, I'm looking forward to a period of less physical activity."

After the meal, they spoke well into the late evening hours. There was a lot to fill her in on, with everything happening in the village. Eventually, exhaustion crept up on her and she asked to be excused. Her bed never felt more comforting to her as she climbed in and pulled the blanket up to her neck. It didn't take long for her to find the land of dreams and she slept the night away.

***

The Final Offering

Just as he promised, Amridon arrived at her home first thing in the morning. Her parents were already out for the day and she had nothing other than him to spend her time on, it was her day to waste. She had already dressed and seemed almost eager when she opened the door. "Well aren't you a timely fella?" She grinned. "Not that I'm complaining."

He smiled back at her. "I couldn't get over here fast enough. Even though we spent the last two months together—as much as a couple can be together during training, that is—but it wasn't enough. I ached to be in your company."

She stood on the tips of her toes and kissed him. "I know exactly what you mean." She closed the door, before turning to him, "Shall we?"

He motioned for her to lead the way. He grabbed her hand, and they headed into the city village. Anticipating a long stroll, she brought a bag and stuffed it as they visited the vendors in the town commons, gathering fresh produce and other tasty. She leaned in closer and reveled in the comfort of his strong arms. They enjoyed the alone time and soaked up every second—they could be a couple for once. He shared about one of the vendor's mothers and she laughed before reaching into her bag to grab a fresh berry, placing it gently in his mouth as he leaned in closer for a kiss. She savored the tart sweetness as the juice collected in his mouth and crossed over to hers. It was the only way to enjoy fresh produce, in her opinion.

With their bag filled with enough food to create a satisfying lunch, they sought solace, a place where they could be alone and in private. They climbed down several branches and walked across the large expanse. She chose a lower bough because it was longer and made crossing to the neighboring aspen tree all the easier. Once on the aspen, they climbed high enough to get a view of the mountain range to the west.

Thula spread a blanket on the branch and pulled out the food. He sat down next to her and lay his head in her lap. It was just like old times between them. She couldn't get over how different he acted when he was away from training. He seemed focused and direct the past two months, fixated on war, even exuberant at killing another. She hated how it turned him into someone she didn't want to be around. Yet, when they were alone, he became the sweet, gentle man she had grown up with; the man she loved. At least he calmed down his aggressive nature since their talk—around her anyway, which was all that mattered.

They sat in silence for several moments. She pondered how much her life changed in just a short time. A couple months ago, she had wondered what her future held. She didn't know where she headed, nor had she cared—she wasn't of age yet, anyway.

Now, she had a job—not to mention a career—and it was something she never anticipated. More than anything, she never expected to be so good at it. She smiled with a sense of pride at what she accomplished and only hoped her original hunches about the elders were incorrect. So far, she hadn't seen suspicious—just ordinary recruit training—and only hoped it held.

A sudden moment of realization came across her mind. *What am I doing?* She thought. Her mind had wandered to useless thoughts when she should have been concentrating on this wonderful moment stretched out before her.

The Final Offering

He smiled and looked deep into her eyes as he asked, "What are you thinking?"

She was caught and tried to steer him away from it. "Oh, nothing. Just pondering the mysterious path we stumbled across." She looked down into his eyes. "What's on your mind?"

He offered a wide grin. "Just staring at your beautiful face and wondering how I got so lucky."

Not sure how to respond, she blushed. Someone crept up behind them. Amridon reached for a weapon, but not anticipating any trouble on this outing, there was no weapon at his disposal. He stood and spun to see who approached. Thula watched as he relaxed when he recognized who it was and his lips spread into a brilliant smile, revealing his bright, white teeth.

Alais and Myriani walked forward. Myriani, always the most vocal of the trio said, "There you two are. We've been looking for you all morning."

Thula stood and ran to her friends, hugging each one. She hadn't spent any time with them on her earlier visits home and longed for their companionship. It was on her list to make time for both of them, eventually; but she hadn't planned on it so soon. At once, she found their presence comforting, although it would mean her afternoon with Amridon would be cut short.

"It is so nice to see you both. You have no idea how much I've missed you guys," Thula said. She dragged them both over to her blanket as Amridon rolled his eyes. "Come sit. Join us." She gazed at the man she loved.

"We have enough food to share." He nodded in agreement. The look on his face told her this wasn't the afternoon he hoped for either, but being the loving man he was, he agreed her friends should join them. Alais and Myriani didn't seem at all bothered by interrupting the two lovebirds. Thula tried to guide the conversation in a different direction. "Tell us what we've missed."

They were surprised when Alais jumped into a rapid succession of recapping what had happened over the past several weeks. "Nothing really. There have been no more Grimmox sightings, and near as any of us can tell, the elders have remained quiet." She looked at Myriani. "In fact, it has been eerily calm ever since they went back into seclusion. It's as if nothing ever happened—except for your training."

"Nothing ever seems to change in our little village," Myriani said, casting a meaningful glance at Alais.

There was something the two of them weren't saying, but they were coy about it. With a quick glance, she checked to see of Amridon picked up on it too, but he seemed oblivious. "What else? I can tell you're not telling me everything. I'm a big girl. Whatever it is, I can handle it," she said.

Alais shrugged and wrapped her arms around Myriani. "Well…" they both locked eyes, before she continued, "Myriani and I have declared our love for one another."

Thula's eyes opened wide, and they definitely had Amridon's attention now. "Congratulations," the pair said in unison.

Thula loved there was no prejudice among the Haloti when it came to same-sex relationships. In the eyes of Halothias, they

The Final Offering

were all God's children, and whatever made them happy, made him happy. This wasn't the case among all the races of the planet, but Thula was glad the Haloti accepted it.

Thula should have already seen this, and she couldn't have been happier for her friends. If anything, it all made sense now. A moment of clarity filled her eyes as she thought back to their childhood. Her friends had always seemed interested in boys—they would always talk in hushed voices and giggle when a cute boy was around—but they never acted upon it and encouraged Thula instead. *Hindsight's twenty-twenty,* she thought.

Excited for them, she wanted more. "How did it happen? I mean, when did you realize? I want all the details!"

Myriani beamed with delight. "It's as if I have always known. There has been this connection between the two of us ever since we were children," she said. "After you and Amridon declared your love for one another, it got us both thinking. Then you left, and we found we had a lot of time alone together."

"I never knew how she felt about me and was afraid to ask. One day, shortly after you left, I found I could no longer contain my feelings for her, and I summoned all the courage I could, leaned over, and kissed her," Alais added, clearly self-satisfied.

"I saw her soft lips moving in my direction and my heart filled with elation. I don't come off this way, but I am quite shy when it comes to love. Had she not made the first move, I doubt anything ever would have come of it." Myriani again let her eyes drift back to Alais. "I've found a comfort with her, and it seems as though I have found a home."

Alais leaned forward and pressed her lips against Myriani's. This was the first time they displayed their affection publicly, and Thula felt honored it was in front of them, their best friends.

Amridon chuckled. "Alais made the first move? I have to admit, I'm surprised. She's always been the shy and passive one."

"When I see something I want, all of that gets thrown out the window," Alais said with a wide grin and a wink.

"Do you think anything more will come of this? I mean, are you going to be sealed?" Thula asked.

"I don't know if we're ready to think about such things now." Myriani shrugged. "We're young and just taking it slow. We'll see what the future holds when we get a little older."

Thula felt a momentary sting at the comment, as though it was a jab at her. She, after all, wouldn't get into a relationship with Amridon until they had spoken to their parents first. After she thought about it for a moment, she reconsidered. Her friends would never mean to be unkind. With a smile, she said, "I'm ecstatic for you guys, I truly am."

She could tell Alais was growing nervous from all the attention as she tried to change the subject. "Enough about us, though. Tell us more. We want to hear all about your training."

Thula and Amridon took turns retelling their version of the eight long weeks of training. They carried on as night drew near, and Thula was glad she grabbed so much produce. They quickly neared the end of the basket. She found she tired of talking since it was all she had been doing since she returned home.

The Final Offering

Amridon's voice relaxed her. So much so, she stretched her body and listened on he continued with their story.

The Final Offering

Chapter 9

The third day after arriving home brought vicious thunderstorms. Lightning stretched across the sky like sharp blades crashing against each other, illuminating the darkness with brilliant white flashes. Although it was morning, there wasn't much light inside. Thula lit a candle whose orange glow flickered and danced with the gentle breeze blowing in through the window, creating moving shadows on the walls of her room.

She had spent so much time with her friends and Amridon that she ached for a little time alone and wanted this morning for herself. With a thick book, she curled up on her bed and read with a blanket wrapped close around her body to ward off the constant draft. Her sister Trana had sent word she wanted to meet her for lunch. She already figured what the topic would be and was regretful she didn't have any information for her.

Lost in her story she laid back in the dimness of her room. Her room illuminated in a bright flash as lightning crashed nearby and the thunder accompanying it shook the thick trunk of the tree. The loud crash brought her out of her trance when she finally realized what time it was. She needed to meet her sister within the hour. With a sigh, she sullenly returned the book to a shelf in her room and changed into more presentable clothes.

The rain hadn't let up, so she grabbed a cloak and tied it around her neck before stepping outside. To protect her hair, she pulled the hood over her head before beginning the climb up the tree. Her sister didn't want to meet in an establishment, so she arranged for them to meet in a hollow of the tree where a branch had broken off several years before. It wouldn't get them out of the wind completely, but would at least protect them from the rain, and Thula thought, any prying ears.

The path leading up the tree had grown slippery from the unrelenting rain of the morning and she had to step with caution, but she eventually made it to the rendezvous point. There was no sign of her sister, so she climbed into the hollow and removed her cloak. The rain soaked the fabric and she would catch a cold if she left it on. Although the biting chill of the wind brought shivers from her exposed skin, at least she was dry. She found a knot to sit on and patiently waited for her sister's arrival.

The rain continued to fall as she almost gave up hope and headed home when her sister's voice broke through the wind. "Thula. Are you up there?"

The Final Offering

She stood up, impatience written all over her face, and said, "Trana! It's about time. I almost gave up on you."

Trana came close to her sister and smiled. Thula was about to offer a hug, when she realized how wet she was and instead waited for her sister to remove her cloak, before embracing her.

"Sorry. It is so nice to see you." Trana stepped back. "The branches were slippery, which slowed my progress. And I felt as though someone was following me, so I took a circuitous path to get here. Please accept my apologies." She grabbed her sister's wrists and gave them a brief squeeze.

Thula nodded in understanding before finally returning her sister's smile. "Why would someone be following you? I thought you were being careful." She looked at her sister with worried eyes. "I hope you're not in any trouble."

"No, I'm sure everything is fine. I'm probably being paranoid." She smiled, but Thula thought it was forced.

"So tell me all about your training. I want to hear everything."

She sighed and retold the story. At this point, she had become downright sick of reliving it, but with such a new program, people were eager to get all the details and she acquiesced.

"Well, that sounds boring." Trana frowned. "Nothing else happened? I mean, you didn't discover any more information? You're right in the thick of it, Thula. I expected you to have at least something to report."

Thula scowled across the expanse at her sister. "I don't know what to tell you. I was very skeptical going in, and on constant alert for anything out of the ordinary. But, as it turns out, there was nothing to be worried about." She caught her sister staring off into the distance in a distracted manner. "That doesn't mean I've given up. When I return, I'm sure I will be much closer to the action. If there is anything to be discovered, I'll find it."

"I sure hope so," Trana said with just a hint of agitation in her voice. "I can tell you, they are up to something. Most people think the elders have gone back into seclusion for meditation, but we've been watching. They're very secretive with their movements—primarily moving during the twilight hours—but we haven't figured out where they are going in the middle of the night."

Thula frowned. She expected this conversation, and she had been dreading it. Her sister expected information and didn't like the answers she gave. "If it makes you feel any better, my plan hasn't changed. I will still keep my eyes open. If I see anything, I will relay it to you. I should be privy to more now that I have rank."

"I know," Trana said with uneasiness in her voice. "I hoped you would've had something for us." She looked up and shook her head. "Sorry, you're trying. It's just, well, something's not right."

Thula wanted to spend quality time with her sister, but it wouldn't happen if they kept on their current course. "So, what else have you been up to? Certainly, you're not concerned only with this precarious situation?"

The Final Offering

"I know what you're trying to do, and I can't say I appreciate it," her sister said with a steel tongue.

"Come now, is there a man in your life? A woman?" she asked with a smile creasing her lips.

"Grow up, Thula." She furrowed her brow. "We're facing possibly the worst crisis our race has ever faced, and you want to ask me about my relationship status?"

"I'm just trying to lighten the mood." Thula offered a smile. "I enjoy talking with you, but I have nothing else to offer, in terms of the elders."

Trana fumed but seemed to agree to let it go—although it was evident she wasn't happy about it.

"I saw your friends in the Commons the other day. They seem happy." She smirked. "At first it caught me off guard, but the more I thought about, the more I felt as though I had always known this would be their path. Have you seen them?"

"Yes, we spoke the other day, but you haven't answered my question. Have you been seeing anyone?"

Trana finally relaxed and grinned sheepishly as she said, "I've been seeing a couple." She chuckled.

Thula breathed a sigh of relief. Her sister finally relaxed and started acting as they did as children. Their talk outlasted the rain and ran well into the afternoon. When Trana said, she had to go, Thula reluctantly stood and embraced her in a hug. They promised to meet each other again before the week was out.

J.G. Gatewood

Thula watched her sister disappear up the tree before she began the climb down, heading back toward her parents' home.

The Final Offering

Chapter 10

The time had finally come, and of course, the week had flown by too quickly. Thula finished packing her bags and made her way downstairs to enjoy one last meal with her parents. Amridon planned to meet her within the hour, and soon they would begin the trek back to the barracks to begin the next phase of their training.

When she entered the kitchen, she saw her mother busy cooking, putting the final touches on their breakfast. The scents of warm cinnamon, apples, and spices tickled her nostrils and brought a thick coating of saliva to her mouth. The apple pastries were her favorite breakfast dish her mother made, and she appreciated the gesture greatly. She walked up to her mother and kissed her cheek. "Good morning. Is there anything I can do to help you?"

Her mother grinned. "No, just take a seat next to your father. We want to enjoy what little time we have left with you."

She walked over and hugged her father, savoring his musky scent, before she took the seat to his left. "You have to stop going to so much trouble on my account," she said to her mother. "But I'm so glad you did."

Her father looked up and beamed at her. "We just... we're so proud of you, Thula. You're too young to be doing the job you're doing, but you're excelling at it. We wanted to send you off with our love and support, oh, and your mother's wonderful cooking in your belly."

"Well, thank you," she said as her mother offered her a freshly cut piece of the pastry on a brown clay plate. She looked up into her mother's eyes and she sniffed before smiling. "It smells divine."

Her mother watched as she ate the first bites of her pastry and let her revel in it before she said, "It's hard to be away. I wanted to give you something good before you're forced to return to the boring food they serve you during training." She thought for a moment while Thula stuffed more into her mouth. "I hope they let you come home more often now that you have proved yourself and are no longer a trainee."

"I'm not sure what our schedule will be yet, but I share the same wish as you. It became lonely being so far away, even though deep down I realize I'm really not that far away." She shrugged and shoveled more into her mouth.

Her mother nodded, but her father spoke. "Keep focused, Thula. We're never that far away and you don't really have much to worry about. We'll always be here. You need to keep

The Final Offering

your head fixed on the task and keep doing your best and remember why you're there."

"Yes, father. I will." She lowered her eyes and continued eating.

A knock came at the door, and she figured it had to be Amridon. As eager as she was to be in his company, she felt sad to leave her family once again.

Her father opened the door and let Amridon into their home. He was very gracious, but Thula could tell they needed to go. She hugged her parents and gathered her bags.

Gorven took Amridon off to the side. "I realize she made it through basic training, but I have a feeling things will become more difficult." Amridon nodded in agreement. "One day you may be sealed with one another, but I ask you to take care of her and protect her now as if you were already fully committed in the holy way of our people."

Amridon smiled. "I will do everything in my power, sir. You will see her returned safely."

Gorven patted him on the back before he ushered them both out the door. Thula gave one last hug to each of them and did her best to keep her emotions in check. They turned and began the climb up the tree with her parents watching them disappear.

When they were out of their view, she turned to Amridon and asked, "What did my father tell you?"

"He's just worried about you, Thula. I reassured him you can take care of yourself."

"Thanks. At least someone knows I'm capable of taking care of myself."

She laid her head on his shoulder as they adopted a leisure pace up to a higher level of the tree. The wind picked up and ruffled her hair. It was an overcast morning with the sun held prisoner behind a thick cover of white clouds. The air was still cool and felt empty and deserted as if they were the only ones moving; although this wasn't the case.

They took their time and wasted several hours, wishing to delay their arrival if only for a time. Before too long, though, they approached the barracks. Several soldiers sat at tables to check each one of them in before ushering them back into the dimly lit room that would serve as their home for the next several weeks.

Thula stowed her belongings and adorned her uniform before heading to the dining hall to grab a bite to eat. She selected an empty table and ate her lunch. After a week of eating her mother's home cooking, she became spoiled. She got it all down though, knowing she would need her energy and the calories packed into the meal to prepare herself.

Amridon and Ploura joined her as she pushed more of the boring food into her mouth.

"We're not even back an hour and I find you stuffing your face," Amridon said. They each took a seat on opposite sides of her.

"You're one to talk. You're down here too," she said. She couldn't help but notice the smirk on his face, but let her gaze wander the hall and the soldiers gathered at the tables. "Is it always like this?"

The Final Offering

Ploura followed her eyes. "Is what always like this?" he asked.

"Look around you. The other soldiers, they are staying away from us. It's like we're diseased or something."

Amridon laughed. "You'll have to get used to it, Thula."

"Why?" She shrugged. "They were all so friendly before."

"You're a higher rank than them now. They no longer view you as an equal." Ploura said.

Amridon reached over and put his arm around her. "Don't worry. It'll get easier."

"I sure hope so. I mean, I expected a small divide, or for something to be a little different, but I didn't expect complete segregation."

"I felt similarly when we all began basic training, except in reverse. I went from holding the rank of corporal to suddenly being a private again. I found it disturbing at first, but it quickly passed." Amridon paused as he looked around the room. "In a way, it was refreshing as if a great weight lifted off my shoulders. But alas, back to the real world, and all the responsibility that comes with it."

Ploura stared at Amridon. Excitement filled his face as he said, "So what do you think they have in store for us? I can't even sleep, I'm so excited."

Amridon scoffed. "It sounds like a lot of classwork. My guess is it will all be boring." His eyes brightened. "Until we get to combat training, that is."

There was the man Thula had come to know and not necessarily enjoy—bored by the monotony of classwork—eager for combat. She saw the spark in his eyes as his other personality re-emerged, and she sunk back in her chair.

With an expressionless face, she sat and watched them both interact. They were both animated and talked of their longing for battle, and she couldn't find the strength to be interested. Their combative and aggressive words fell on her deaf ears, and she stared off in thought as they continued their banter.

Amridon made a crude joke about the Grimmox and burst out in laughter. She decided she had had enough and excused herself. Amridon's eyes shot towards hers as if to ask if there was anything he had done. Although she felt differently, she shook her head and tried to show everything was all right but didn't speak to him. She calmly walked out of the hall.

The evening air was cool and refreshing on her skin and lifted her spirits. It had only been half a day and already missed her parents. Her mother's cooler head and her father's sense of what was right and wrong was just what she needed right now to calm her. Just the thought of them brought clarity and control to her mind, but also a pang of homesickness.

Lifting her head she looked at the sky, and the twinkling stars brought a smile to her face. The gentle breeze brushing across her face delighted her and felt like the softness of feathers tickling her soft skin. She took a deep breath and listened as nature spoke to her. The chorus of crickets surrounded her; a symphony of chirping lulled her and put her in a trance as she made her way out on the branch. The sights and sounds reminded her of long summer nights sitting out in the open air,

The Final Offering

taking it all in. Before long, she forgot all about her uneasiness from earlier.

At a junction of two branches, she sat and dangled her legs, staring down and wondering what kind of life the Grimmox lived. She had never seen one herself but wondered how two species who shared a tree could be so different. Of course, all she believed was only what she had been told—she hoped none of it was true. In her heart, she wanted the stories to be wrong. She wanted peace and prosperity for the two races. And why not? They had existed peacefully thus far. There was no reason to hate them. While the stories of the two fairies' history together were indeed ingrained in them all, so was the inherent need to respect, if not love, all of God's creations. Didn't that include their fellow tree fairies?

She only wished there was something more she could do to make sure this became a reality. Thinking long and hard about it, little by little her nervous thoughts shifted to their upcoming training.

Movement on the branch below caught her attention, and she squinted to make out who it was. Through her narrowed eyes, she spotted a figure walking with a limp. It wore a red, silk cloak pulled close to the individual's skinny, frail body. Whoever it was, they had to be old. With no further thought, she gazed over the valley stretched out before her, but her eyes caught and focused on a glimpse of scraggly, white hair from within the red hood and she watched the mysterious being once again. It dawned on her in an instant, *an elder,* she thought. Every instinct told her to follow them, but she suspected they would be too aware of that. She struggled with what to do. Her whole world and the thoughts she had been having about the situation seemed to turn upside down as she contemplated the meaning behind their presence at the training facility.

Suddenly unnerved, she walked back to her quarters—her mind raced with angry and curious thoughts, but she couldn't risk jumping the gun. She needed to think this through before she did anything rash. There was no reason an elder should be here. It didn't seem normal and her senses tingled. Her first night back would be anything but restful.

The Final Offering

Chapter 11

After a night filled with tossing and turning, Thula walked out of the barracks and stretched her back in the bright morning sunlight. Shooting pains shot through her nerve endings and she remembered the night's restlessness. *It will be a long day if this keeps up,* she thought as she stretched. Her thoughts meandered as she saw two squirrels fighting over an acorn farther down the tree and stole her attention. They bickered back and forth when she suddenly realized she would be late if she didn't get a move on it.

Her training would begin on the next branch higher. She hadn't been excited about all the *rumored* classwork, but on this morning, she was grateful. Upset by the events from the previous evening her stomach churned, she hadn't eaten anything.

The classroom sat filled with several of the new soldiers when she walked in and surveyed the tables. Students already filled most of the desks—and of course, Amridon had selected a spot right up front—but she found one in the back and made her way over to it. She smiled at a soldier seated to her right and took a deep breath. The air was thick in her lungs and tasted stale—the room felt stuffy and claustrophobic. She understood why when she looked around and couldn't find any windows. Ready for the training to begin, she sighed and sunk back into her chair.

For the next few moments, the soldiers made small talk with one another as they waited for their instructor. Similar to the night before, most people ignored her, leaving her to wallow in her own self-doubt. Finally, a sergeant walked in and the room quieted. She recognized him and followed him with narrowed eyes.

He strode to the podium and cleared his throat. "Welcome. I am Sergeant Monda. I would like to congratulate you all on your successful completion of basic training." He looked around the room. "I'm told several of you excelled. It's a pleasure to be in the company of so many highly regarded soldiers."

He left the safety of the podium and with an air of confidence paced back and forth in front of the room. "I know we're in a classroom," he stretched out his hands to emphasize his statement, "and some of you expect the next phase to be easy. Let me tell you how incorrect those thoughts are. This will be the most difficult undertaking you've experienced thus far." Many of the soldiers exchanged glances filled with uncertainty.

The Final Offering

"You will learn every day while in the program. Several teachers will be here to guide you. When you leave, you'll be expected to continue your studies on your own time, and you'll be tested. A single failure will result in your expulsion from the program, so I expect you to take this seriously."

He raised his voice to punctuate his next point. "If you don't think you can handle it, there is the door." He pointed. "You've all passed basic training and we will gladly enroll you in another program. I'm serious about this, espionage is not for everyone. Only the smartest will excel, and just because you complete the studies required, doesn't guarantee you a continued spot in the program. We only want the best. You're expected to eat, drink, study, and even dream everything Grimmox."

Several of the new soldiers stared at the sergeant in fear. His words weren't that harsh—even though clearly this was what the sergeant wanted—but they were enough to bring a couple to their feet where they shamefully walked out the door. The already thick air grew denser—enough that one could imagine cutting through it with a knife. The remaining soldiers perked up in their seats and paid even more attention to Monda.

Turned back to his students, he smiled. "Now that we weeded out some of your weaker compatriots, we can continue. This program will teach you more about our enemy." Thula cringed at the harsh use of the word for their seemingly peaceful tree-mates.

"The Grimmox are a nasty, hateful group of individuals who would like nothing more than our extermination." His words hung in the heavy air. "More than that though, they're crafty. Before a couple weeks ago, a Grimmox hadn't ventured into our territory for several generations, but don't let that fact mislead you. This isn't because they haven't been spying on us, trust me, they have. They're just good at it. They've been doing it for millennia and have learned how to blend in with their surroundings. Alongside your studies, we will conduct classes in the art of how to do the same. When we are done with you, your presence will never be noticed, nor even suspected. You'll be just another fly on the wall, an invisible set of eyes and ears, and that is exactly what we expect of you."

The sergeant returned to the podium. "Along the way, we will welcome several guest instructors who will aid in your education. Today, we've been blessed enough to have an elder in our presence. She has more experience with the Grimmox than anyone else in our village."

Wait, a minute... she? Thula thought. That's *who I saw last night.* The elder shuffled into the room wearing a dark, red cloak.

The elder walked with a limp, but still owned a confidence befitting her station as she made her way to the podium. The elder paused a moment at the front of the classroom, then removed her hood, revealing the aged, dark face of elder, Silonia. Her face was well weathered and wrinkled. Although her skin was darker than most, her age spots were visible. Her skin was loose and slack, almost hanging from the bone and appearing as though it were melting off her face. At least Thula now understood whom she had seen the night before.

"Thank you, sergeant, for the fine introduction." The voice was raspy and hoarse as she nodded toward the sergeant, before addressing the soldiers. "We live in a day and age that is trying, and probably the most dangerous we've seen in generations.

The Final Offering

The Grimmox represent the greatest threat we've ever faced and the time of inaction has passed.

"Since the early days of our race, we've lived in fear. A fear that began the very day the Grimmox banished us to the farthest reaches of the tree. You would think this would've satisfied their vindictive hearts. But no, they barred us from traveling to the ground through their lands. The most heinous crime the Grimmox is responsible for is the annual offering they forced us to agree to.

"For hundreds of years, we've lost one of our young. They've just been handed over to the beasts, never to be seen or heard from again. Who knows what kind of torture they've been subjected to, the many secrets they've been forced to give up. Their lives have been wasted before they ever even had a chance to really begin. And for what?

"This is a question I've been asking myself for quite some time. Ever since the Grimmox broke our agreement I've been bothered by what we have allowed to transpire throughout our long history. I soon switched to anger, and something needed to be done.

"They spread the lies we are both the same, just different shades of skin, but don't believe it, not for a second. Sure we may appear alike, but that's where our similarities end. They even refuse to treat Halothias as a god. They instead accept the word of Grimosias, his brother, who lied when he said although they were the sons of God, it didn't make them gods in their own right." Silonia snickered.

Elder Silonia's enthusiasm gained fervor from the soldiers in the room. "That's right, there is no lie this evil species won't tell. They've used them to keep us at bay for generations. But their complete disrespect for our agreement has shown me it is time we no longer live in fear. We will call them on their lies, and we will hold them accountable for all the children they've robbed from us throughout the years."

Several of the soldiers stood from their chairs and threw up their arms in applause as raucous cheers exploded, shaking the walls as the sound reverberated around the room.

Thula's mouth dropped open in shock. *I don't understand this.* She had, of course, heard several of these rumors all her life, but never did she think they would be used as a call to war. Any unpleasant thoughts or reservations she had about their entire situation soon formulated into a single concrete feeling. If she didn't know any better, she would think the elder was trying to brainwash them. The worst part was it seemed to work. She looked around at the naivety of her unit, shaking her head in disappointment as the elder continued.

"Who here has lost a loved one to the offering?" She looked around the room. Thula followed her eyes hoping, no, praying that no one would raise a hand. Unfortunately, one hand shot up in the back of the room.

Silonia shook her head somberly. "What a shame. May I ask the name of your lost loved one?"

"Her name was Linessa." A soldier with dark blonde hair said in a harsh whisper.

With exaggerated empathy, Silonia nodded. Thula saw right through her ruse. "Linessa. What a lovely name. I remember her." She took a couple steps forward. "Was she your sister?"

The Final Offering

"Aye, she was." The soldier nodded. "And taken too young, she was. Only fourteen years old, her life cut short." The pain of the loss filled his voice.

"Much too young," Silonia agreed. "Wouldn't you like to avenge her? Take out your frustration on those who've caused you so much pain?"

"That's the reason I'm here. I never had any inkling to join the military, but when the opportunity presented itself I knew what I had to do." His teeth gritted and Silonia smiled.

"That's what we have to remember. Maybe they weren't impacted directly throughout the years, but we have a duty to protect our children. They're our children, brothers, sisters, or even our cousins, and they deserve the right to live their lives without the same fears we've all grown up with. This ritual is barbaric and we're finally in a position where we can put a stop to it, right here, right now." Another standing ovation ensued.

Thula looked over her shoulder to gauge Amridon's response and her heart sank, as he seemed to be just as engrossed in the lies of this old woman as the rest of them appeared to be. Her mouth grew dry and her stomach churned, sending a small amount of acid up her throat. She swallowed it back down but cringed as the bitterness filled her mouth.

She knew the history as well as any, and it wasn't as though she was supportive of the Grimmox, nor their mistreatment of the Haloti, but she didn't agree with their use to breed hatred and spread dissent throughout their otherwise peaceful nation.

With bated breath, Amridon sat on the edge of his seat, hanging on to every one of the elder's words as Silonia continued to spew her rhetoric. Thula did her best to tune the old woman out as she tried to process.

After hours of evocative bashing of the other species, and endless descriptions of how beastly and vile they acted, she finally came to an end, and Thula breathed a sigh of relief. If the whole program would be this way, it would be a long two months.

She walked out into the fresh air, hit by a blast of heat. It was mid-afternoon, and the air felt calm and dry. Amridon stood with several of his friends and waved her over, but after how he had acted in class, she had no intention of joining him and waved him off. He looked slightly concerned at first, but quickly became engrossed in their jovial conversation.

The Final Offering

Chapter 12

After a long week of what she now referred to as "The Brainwashing Sessions," they added another class to their daily routine. They were learning hand-to-hand combat. No weapons were allowed and the new skills helped take her mind off all the nonsense the elder preached to them day after day. Of course, the chance to burn off some of her frustration from the other classes didn't hurt matters either.

She watched as two soldiers parried and dodged one another, bounding from branch to branch, using nothing but their hands as weapons. Crouched on her legs, she itched for this battle to conclude so she could get in on the action. One of the soldiers used his wings and launched himself into the air, carrying him up two more branches.

As her eyes followed the maneuver, she spotted someone in a window up above. She didn't want to stare and risk bringing attention to herself, so she did her best to identify the watcher by staring out of the corner of her eye.

Silonia, she thought. *Odd that she would be watching this phase of the training.* Stranger still was that it appeared she was trying to watch her. Thula was afraid she might be attracting too much attention and decided to keep her eyes open.

Refocused on the battle in front of her, it appeared Norfin had the upper hand in the fight. He was bigger than his opponent, and the poor sap couldn't counter Norfin's moves. However, just because he wasn't as big as Norfin, didn't mean he wasn't gifted with strengths of his own; he was much faster and agiler. *He needs to use his speed to his benefit*, but it didn't seem he knew how. Before she could think further about it, Norfin had him pinned to the ground and his opponent yelled out his surrender, much to the applause of the others, and chagrin of the instructor.

She wasn't at all surprised to hear her name called next, but she hadn't expected her opponent. Amridon strolled up with a wide grin on his face.

They faced each other on the long branch as a hush fell over the assembled crowd. Eying one another she couldn't help but notice the smirk on his face. It was difficult, but she didn't show any emotion—it was, after all, one of the tricks they were supposed to be practicing. The instructor motioned for them to begin and she immediately started moving right. Amridon countered and moved to his right. They circled, each waiting for the other to make a move. The soldiers stepped back to give them more room.

The Final Offering

"I bet you never thought it would come down to a battle between us," he called to her, his smirk broadening to a grin. "Show me what you've got. What're you waiting for?"

Now she did show emotion and smiled. "For you to show your opening move," she said. He mistakenly offered an opening, and she ran at him before he had a chance to adjust. He tried to position himself in her path, but she surprised him and jumped. With the help of her wings, she flew over him, spinning in a flip, and twisted at the last second, her foot connecting with his back. Before he could regain his position, she landed on him and settled a well-timed punch to his head. A giddiness filled her, even though she didn't show it.

She jumped back and let him get to his feet. A small hint of anger flashed in his eyes. As she waited for him to retaliate, she spotted Silonia still peering at her through her window. Not wanting to become too distracted, she refocused on Amridon who ran right at her. Anticipating what he intended to do—also knowing what her normal response would be—she tried something different. He lunged at her with his arm ready to swing. Her first instinct was to try to move to the side to parry, but she instead used her speed to drop to the ground on her back. Using his weight against him, she pulled him forward and used her feet to flip him over her own body, where he crashed to the ground. Several people applauded, but she didn't have any time to acknowledge them. She ran to him and landed on him with her elbow.

With a grin where only he could see her, she said, "Had enough yet?" The words only antagonized him more.

Still, on his back, he wiped a slow trickle of blue blood away from his lip and said, "I'm only getting started." He snarled as he moved his feet under her ribcage. With them in position, he kicked and sent her flying onto her own back.

Back on his feet, he lunged at her. She counted off the time in her head and waited for the perfect opportunity. Just as he was about to connect with a fist, she rolled to the side and out of the way. He grunted from the impact and she winced as a sudden pain ripped up her side.

Ignoring the pain, she adopted a crouched, defensive posture, waving him forward and encouraging him to charge. Taunting was never a good idea with him, but she couldn't believe how well she had done so far and wanted to continue to put on a good show.

She countered his next two moves, sneaking in a few of her own successful blows and turned to await his attack. Several new bruises adorned her otherwise perfect skin and her body reeled with pain. Sweat trickled down her forehead and stung her eyes, but she didn't dare risk wiping it away as it would take her eyes off her opponent.

One look at Amridon was enough to convince her she was wearing him out too. Confident she was doing everything her instructors had trained her to do, she just felt bad it had to come at the expense of her boyfriend, and she had no doubt she would hear about it later.

In one last exhausted attempt, he ran toward her. She saw it coming and rolled to the side. The bones in her shoulders cracked as they made contact with the branch, and she used her momentum to carry her back to her feet. Jumping on his back, she wrapped her arms around his neck to cut off his air supply. He spun, flailing his arms wildly as he tried to get her off. His

The Final Offering

eyes bulged in their sockets, and he threw all his weight back and crashed to the branch, crushing her beneath him.

The breath rushed out of her lungs in a massive gasp. Struggling to draw in fresh air, her limbs grew numb as the muscles were deprived of the much-needed supply of oxygen. Through it all though, she managed to maintain and even increase the pressure with her arms around his neck. Not willing to relent, the words she had been waiting for finally came.

Through clenched teeth, he said, "I yield."

She relaxed her grip, and they both struggled to get back on their feet. Walking gingerly, she joined the rest of her class, doing her best to keep her excitement contained.

Thula spent the rest of the afternoon watching the rest of her companions face off in combat as the muscles in her arms, legs and back tightened. She was impressed by several of the soldiers in her unit, but she quickly grew bored.

They were excused, starved from their exertions they all made their way directly to the dining hall to fill their stomachs without any further thought of cleaning up or changing clothes.

Thula wasted no time herself and grabbed a plate. She eyed Amridon and offered a smirk as she called him over, but he turned his back. He selected a seat with a couple of his friends. It hurt and bothered her he would act in such a manner. Obviously, this behavior came back to previously beating him in hand-to-hand combat. But what was she supposed to do, loose on purpose? That wasn't her way, had never been her way, and she wasn't about to change now.

She sulked as she sat down at an empty table when several other soldiers waved her over. After weeks of them ignoring her, it felt good to have their respect as though she had done something to bridge that gap. She accepted and joined them, selecting the last seat at the table. Amridon noticed, but ignored the act just the same.

"That was amazing. How did you beat Amridon?"

Thula blushed. "We grew up together. We've played around, fighting as children will do, since we were young. Many of the things he tried when he was younger have carried over to his fighting style as an adult. It was easy to anticipate what he would do next."

"But where did you learn how to fight? It seemed so natural to you, yet you only received the same training the rest of us did. I mean, Amridon is so much larger than you."

She shrugged her shoulders. "My father always wanted a son. As the third daughter in the family, he raised me as though I were a boy. I mean, I've been hunting since I could pull back a string," she said.

"I guess it suits you well. You're going to make one heck of a soldier."

Suddenly Thula's smile disappeared. She knew the comment was meant as a compliment, but she never intended to make this a career. Worry filled her, and she started thinking maybe this would be the best her life had in store.

She finished her dinner and excused herself from the table. The company was nice, but the revelations of the evening made her uncomfortable. The fresh, crisp evening air brushed her face

The Final Offering

when she walked outside. It helped to clear her mind, and she hoped to put her thoughts into some semblance of order.

She didn't want any interruptions. What she really wanted was some time alone to think. She climbed up several branches of the tree to get a better view of the stars. The moon, now three-quarters full, shined brightly in the black charcoal of the evening sky, illuminating her face. She wondered how she had meandered down this path. She thought she was in love with Amridon, which is why she was here in the first place, but many of his actions made her re-assess the situation. Sometimes he seemed so loving, so doting, almost as if he would do anything for her. But in other situations, he acted like he did today; a stubborn man.

A small sigh escaped her lips, and suddenly she yearned for his companionship. *Why?* She thought. *What can he possibly offer that could atone for his actions today?*

Now she waged an internal war with herself; equal parts wishing he was there to comfort her and then hoping he would just leave her alone. It was all so frustrating. Regardless, she wanted nothing more than for him to come after her tonight. No, she expected it, and she patiently waited for his presence. Her wings fluttered nervously as time ticked by, but as the moon slowly moved across the sky, and the chill of the wind bit into her bones, indicating it was time to give up. She stood and made her way back to the barracks. She changed and washed before climbing into bed.

The Final Offering

Chapter 13

The commander granted the espionage unit a rare afternoon off from training; the commander had other duties to attend to, and since it appeared the soldiers were making good progress, he gave them time to themselves.

Having made several new friends, she spent the afternoon eating lunch with them. No reconciliation had taken place with Amridon, a fact she lamented. He had become very standoffish and steered clear of her most of the time. On the rare occasion where they had time to talk, he seemed cold, leaving her with no way to make any progress. It didn't seem right, but she feared she would need to apologize for the entire incident. The way she attacked him was how she was. How could he blame her for following orders? After a year in the military, he should know it already. Her heart felt empty though, and she wanted him back in her life; the way they used to be… the way it was before all of this other stuff had blurred the lines of their relationship.

At least she had others that made her feel at home now. Friendship went a long way to help heal a broken heart, and it couldn't have come at a better time. She laughed as they ate their sandwiches in the hot afternoon sun. Sunlight trickled through the thick green leaves, fluttering in the strong breeze blowing in from the south. The days were growing shorter now that summer was half over. It wouldn't be too long before the leaves changed color and dropped, littering the ground with a soft blanket. That also meant the offering was right around the corner too, a thought she couldn't seem to keep from her mind.

A light afternoon run was on their schedule and as they made their preparations, a sergeant came up behind them. "I'm looking for Corporal Thula. Is she up here?"

Surprised, she stepped forward. "I'm Thula. What can I help you with?"

He cleared his throat and looked at her, unease filling his face. "You've been summoned to Elder Silonia's quarters."

"Silonia! What does she want from me?" Anxiety creased her face.

"She didn't say, ma'am." He shifted uncomfortably, "If you would follow me."

Thula thanked her friends and followed the soldier. With each step, her feet grew heavier, and what should have been a quick walk felt like an eternity. The attention she had garnered

The Final Offering

from the elder lately only put her more on edge as fear crippled her body. *But I've been so careful,* she thought. *Haven't I?*

The sergeant knocked when they reached Silonia's door. It creaked open, and she walked inside after taking a deep breath. *Here goes nothing!*

"Thula, what a pleasure to meet you. Sorry to pull you away on such short notice. I understand you were given the afternoon off, and I'm sure there are other places you would much rather be." She motioned to the chair. "Please, take a seat."

"Thank you, Elder," she said, awkwardly fidgeting.

The elder sat opposite her on a long couch. "It seems you're excelling in the program. Are you enjoying the training so far?" she asked. Her wrinkled face stretched into a grin. The sunlight cascading through the windows formed shadows under the many lines drawn all over her face by time's hand, making her appear even older than she truly was.

Thula wanted to cringe at her appearance, but to do so might give off the wrong impression, so she bit back her lip and tried her best to keep her composure.

"Yes, it's a natural fit. I can use many of the skills my father taught me when I was a child."

"I don't think that begins to describe it. I watched your fight the other day. Quite impressive." Her eyes grew large, looking as if she might swallow her whole.

Thula blushed and didn't know quite how to respond.

The elder continued. "Yes, quite the fighter." She steepled her fingers and rested her chin on the tips with her eyes narrowing. "Can you see why this presents a dilemma for me?"

"Dilemma? I don't understand what you mean," Thula stuttered.

"Well, let me explain it to you then." The elder stood and walked to the window where she gazed out upon the valley stretching to the east, hands laced behind her back. "You think you've been so smart. So much so, you don't think we really know what's going on." She spun around. "Why did you join this program?"

Unease filled her, and she squirmed in her chair. *How can she know? What are you doing? You're taking too long. Give her an answer.*

"I, um, joined because I was outraged by the encroachment of the Grimmox onto our land." She only hoped this answer would satisfy the old woman's inquiry.

"Your outrage?" The elder walked back to the couch and sat down, eagerness filling her face. "Tell me more about how you were outraged."

I've done it now, she thought. Her mind raced trying to come up with something. Anything she could use to convince the elder.

"What do you mean?" Instead of waiting for her response, she continued on the offensive. "We've all heard the stories. They've been ingrained into our skulls since our early days. They are evil creatures who are determined to rule over the entire tree."

The Final Offering

I can't believe I just said that. Every class, or brainwashing session she attended, had only served to make her question everything more and more. She only hoped she was adding enough inflection to her voice, enough anger to make the elder see that she meant what she was saying.

"The fact they would risk the treaty, a treaty which has been in place for thousands of years, by sending a scout into our lands had my anger bubbling." She paused while she considered her next words.

"We've abided by the treaty, sending one of our own as part of the offering, and for what? For them to cross our borders? Why, it can only mean one thing, an invasion. I signed up as soon as it was offered. To help put right countless generations of wrongdoing." The false words dripped too easily from her tongue. They were ripe with ire and she would never have thought she had it in her. Then again, she had been fed these stories––what she now figured to be lies—her entire life.

Silonia sat back, sinking further into the couch as she listened to Thula's words. "Very interesting, Thula. Tell me, why do you sit quietly through all of my lessons then? You show no emotion with all I am revealing, and unlike the other soldiers in your unit, you seem displeased by my words."

Her lips parted as she began to speak, but was afraid they would betray her. She bit her lip and tried to stay stone-faced as she shrugged.

Silonia leaned forward. "I've thought about it long and hard, and the only answer I keep coming back to is that you're lying." The elder sat back gauging Thula's emotions, which remained stoic. "You're trying to play a little of the double agent. Is that your true intention, Thula?"

It's all over. The elder has seen through everything. How could I have been so stupid? She wondered. Obviously, Silonia was getting too close. She didn't know how to answer, and before she could stop herself, her mouth opened. "Is there something you should be nervous about, Elder?"

Shock registered quick as a crack of thunder and Silonia stood. "How dare you accuse me, or any of the elders for that matter, of doing anything outside of our normal duties?"

"That's just it, Elder, I never accused you of anything. I only asked if there was something you were afraid of," she grinned. Thula was skating on thin ice, but for whatever reason, she couldn't help herself.

Silonia's eyes grew large as she realized her mistake. "Well, yes, I misunderstood you." She offered a fake smile. "Please accept my apologies. I'm only trying to discern whether there is an issue here."

Thula sighed. "There is no issue. Everything I've said is the truth." *Please believe me. I want you to leave me alone.* She grew tired of the conversation and only wanted to go back to her relaxing afternoon. Although, how she could relax now was anyone's question.

"I hope for your sake, they are. If you haven't noticed, we control everything." The elder spread her arms to show the empty space surrounding them. "We are not a group of people whose bad side you want to be on. If what you say is true, you have nothing more to worry about, but remember, we're keeping our eyes on you."

The Final Offering

Thula felt the full weight of the Elder's words rest on her shoulders before Silonia continued. "If you are up to something, be warned. We can either be friends, or we can be enemies. And we have our own ways of taking care of enemies."

This was no thinly veiled threat, and she nodded in understanding. It wasn't difficult for her to remember the old woman escorted from the village common area after voicing her distrust of the elders. "Is there anything else?" She stood to excuse herself from the room.

"Sit back down." Anger flashed across Silonia's face. "I haven't dismissed you yet."

Her wings fluttered in frustration as she retook her chair. Crossing her arms, she gave off an air of agitation.

"See! This is what I am referring to. It is as if my very presence disgusts you. I've seen you and you understand the protocols. I demand that you show a little respect."

Quick, say something. "I'm sorry, it's just that it's my day off. I was enjoying what little free time we get before I was rudely interrupted and brought before you to have my motives questioned. Can't you understand how frustrating that must be? I've done nothing to show I don't believe what I've said. This little meeting has rocked my nerves. I feel like I have put my entire heart into this new program, and frankly, I'm excelling in it."

"That's why the other elders and I are so concerned about your lack of interest in my class, and the history of which I'm expounding upon. You've excelled in the program. And I must admit, you very well may be the most adept and promising recruit to join any of our programs in quite some time. Before we went any further, I just wanted to have a conversation with you to understand where your allegiances lay." Thula thought she almost saw a glimmer of admiration in her eyes. "And I am very sorry for interrupting your free day. It was the only opportunity we had to bring you in for our little chat."

Thula didn't trust the elder's words. "Thank you and I appreciate your time. I'm sorry if my actions have in any way indicated I'm not fully invested in this program, or that I had ulterior motives."

"I thank you for the kind words. Just remember, you've been warned. I'll be watching you." The elder grinned as she stood. "You're free to leave."

Thula bowed, before leaving her chambers. Her body broke out in sweat as she stepped outside and the cool, fresh air hit her face. She leaned against the wall and exhaled, breathing deeply for the first time all afternoon. Tremors overwhelmed her limbs, and she tried her best to calm herself before deciding on a hasty retreat. Taking two steps at a time, she made her way down the tree. A lone branch which was rarely visited, popped into her mind, and she changed directions, seeking the solace offered by the empty limb. Dropping to her knees, she cupped her face as tears streamed from her eyes. Her ragged breathing came in gasps as she tried to regain control.

The rays of the sun filled her eyes and glistened on her wet face. She wanted to scream but was afraid it would call too much attention to herself. *How could I have been so foolish?* She thought. *Of course, they're paying attention to me. It's exactly as Silonia said, my disdain is so visible she has seen right through me. I've been so stupid.*

The Final Offering

She pounded her fist on the branch. It sent a shooting pain up her arm. The pain was a nuisance, but it would serve as a reminder of how she needed to be careful. Lucky was the only word she could think of to describe the events, and she would have to be even more cautious going forward.

She stood, wiped the tears away from her eyes and made her way back toward her barracks. It was still mid-afternoon, but she was so exhausted she collapsed onto her bed. The day's events kept replaying over-and-over in her head as she tried to formulate a plan. Several soldiers from her unit tried to get her to join them for dinner, but she waved them off. Instead, she stayed in bed and wallowed in her own self-pity.

The Final Offering

Chapter 14

As the weeks progressed, she continued to do quite well in her training and continued to receive praise. She had even adjusted her attitude while in Silonia's class, modeling her behavior after others in her unit. It seemed her change in demeanor pleased Silonia, but she was afraid the elder could see through her ploy. With everything that happened, she would never underestimate her, or any of the other elders, ever again.

Only confounding the problem was that she and Amridon seemed to be drifting further apart. It pained her heart, and she yearned for the simpler times before any of this had transpired. Her whole life was thrust into turmoil, and she was playing so many roles, she was having a difficult time remembering who she was. Of course, this is what they were training for. The life of a spy was confusing in and of itself; add in her own secret mission and things easily became muddled. It was as though the real Thula drifted farther and farther away, like a bag caught in the wind, always just out of reach.

As they neared the end of their current phase of training, Amridon surprised her one evening and showed up at her barracks. Hoping she wouldn't regret it, she walked out and met him.

"Amridon, what are you doing here? Shouldn't you be preparing for tomorrow's lesson?"

He grinned and stepped closer. "I came to see you. Can't a boyfriend drop in and surprise his girlfriend once in a while?"

"Of course, it's just... you've never done anything like this." She flashed a weak smile. "At least, not since we've been in training."

The grin slipped from his face. "I've been thinking about that myself. It's frustrating how little one-on-one time we've spent with one another. But I'm trying to change that. At least a little, I hope." He stepped closer to her. "Would you go with me to dinner?" He wrapped his arms around her and hugged her, breathing deeply of her sweet scents.

She backed off, pushing him away. "You know we can't do that, not in this manner at least. What would the other soldiers think?"

He laughed. "No, that's not what I was referring to. I've arranged for a dinner out in our favorite spot. Just you, me, the bright stars of the gods, and the silver moon showering us in a flood of light."

The Final Offering

She had to admit it sounded nice, but was it all too late? He was so enthralled by the idea of revenge, he had almost become a different person; a person she didn't like. Even though she hated the feeling, hadn't she also become a different person? Through all of their training, she operated under her own agenda, one that included deception to the person whom she loved most dearly.

After a moment of thought, she said, "It sounds like the perfect evening." With a quick glance over her shoulder at her barracks to decide if she needed anything else, she said, "Let's go."

They linked their arms together before they made their way to a secluded branch they had visited many times before. A basket of food and a thick blanket awaited them beneath the starry sky. The stars blinked and twinkled in the cool, dry evening air. He motioned for her to sit, and he took his place across from her. A gentle breeze brushed her hair against the smooth features of her face, as it lifted the branch ever so slightly, before settling back to its resting position.

"Thank you for agreeing to go with me. It's been too long since we've been alone." He offered a warm—and what appeared to be—a genuine smile. Her heart warmed as she realized he was being real for the first time in a long time.

"It's my pleasure to spend a little time with you."

He leaned over and kissed her as she wrapped her arms around his muscular body, savoring every moment of the short embrace. After a moment of joy, he pulled back and handed her food from the basket. It was nothing special, just sandwiches and fruit, but she enjoyed it nonetheless.

"So tell me, are you satisfied with the training?" she asked. "It seems you're enjoying yourself and you've done well."

"Quite pleased. Well... except for one instance," he grinned. "You see, there was this one time where I should have dominated my opponent. But she was tricky and unfortunately knew me all too well. Without realizing it, she saw what I was going to do..."

She leaned over and punched his arm playfully.

"Hey, what was that for?" A smile filled his face as he asked the question. "I'm only kidding, of course. In all honesty, I'm surprised at how well you've done. I guess I shouldn't be, but I am."

"Why should you be surprised?" she scoffed. "You've been around me my whole life. You saw firsthand how my father wanted a son, and he raised me as one even though I'm obviously female."

"Yeah, that too has been surprising." He chuckled, and she raised her fist in a joking manner as if she was going to hit him again, but he waved her off. "No need for any more abuse. It's just that because of all of your father's training and treatment, you always somewhat acted like a boy. I would never have expected you to grow into the breathtaking woman you are today." His smile showed his sincerity. "And I'm glad. Even though you didn't always act like a woman, I always found myself attracted to you."

"Thanks," sarcasm dripped from her tongue. "I'm just glad you grew out of your awkward clumsy phase yourself. I never would've remotely considered a courtship with you had you

The Final Offering

continued your bumbling ways." He let out a guffaw in response.

They finished their dinner in relative silence, just enjoying one another's company. Affectionate embraces and handholding replaced the unspoken words between the pair. Nothing needed to be said, things were seemingly back to normal between them. They gazed at the stars and watched the constellations form in the emptiness of space as the night grew darker. The air filled with the chirping of crickets and flashes of fireflies, bringing to mind memories of pictures she saw as a child. It made her feel comfortable and at home.

As their night together wore on, he stiffened and seemed to grow uncomfortable. She could tell something was on his mind, and she waited for him to come right out and say it, to no avail.

"Is something bothering you?" she finally asked. "The night was going along so nicely, but you suddenly seem distracted."

"Oh, it's nothing. I'm just thinking about our next phase of training. You know we'll be training with weapons next week."

"I'm well aware of our schedule, Amridon," she moved her hands to her hips. "Don't try to distract me and don't lie to me either. Something else is going on. What is it?"

He sighed before looking into her eyes. "It's just that something doesn't seem right with you."

Oh no, she thought, *he's going to end our courtship. What have I done wrong?* "What doesn't seem right? Have I done something to upset you?" she asked.

He waved his hands in response. "No, it's nothing you've done to me, what I mean is I noticed a change in you a couple weeks ago. I know you haven't always been happy with the elders, and you disagree with their decision about the Grimmox, but if that is the case then why did you even join the program in the first place?

She exhaled deeply before speaking, she had an odd sensation she needed to choose her words carefully. "No, I don't necessarily agree with the decision of the elders, but then again I don't think the Grimmox are free from fault either. If they encroached on our lands, then they deserve to answer for their misdeeds. But, I don't know if the course we're following is a wise one."

"What then of the elders? Will you follow where they lead? he asked. His voice seemed to have a little more edge, a new coldness to it that sent a shiver down her spine. Something was different with him.

"Their role serves a purpose, but I don't think they should have so much say over what...." She stopped herself, suddenly remembering her recent conversation with Silonia. She should tread lightly with her words. It bothered her that she had to withhold information from him.

"Have so much what? You didn't finish your sentence." Again, his voice was cold and more formal as he pressed her for more information.

Her eyes drifted to the ground. "I will follow the path they lay before me. They speak through the will of Halothias and I will follow as they deem proper." She took a deep breath. *Am I*

The Final Offering

really doing this? Lying right to his face? Her thoughts were a mixed blur of emotions and a need for caution.

"That! Right there! That's exactly what I'm talking about." His voice became very accusatory. "Your whole demeanor has changed. Why?"

"What would you have me do? This is the program I joined, and this is what is expected of me, what all our training is for."

She thought she caught a momentary glimpse of anger flash deep in his eyes. It startled her and almost made her jump. *Where is this coming from? Has someone mentioned something to him? Why, all of a sudden, is he so interested in my views and opinions on why we are here?*

Within seconds, his eyes returned to normal, losing the glint of anger, and her heart started to calm down. He was silent for a moment. "You never answered my question. Everything we're doing, all that we're learning, seems to be in conflict with what you're saying." His voice seemed void of any emotion as if he were suddenly a robot. "Why did you join the program?"

"You know why I joined the program, Amridon." He shook his head and her heart sank even further. "I joined because of you. I wanted to be with you, to make sure you didn't do anything stupid. I wanted to protect you." The hurt in her voice seemed lost on the man who was supposed to be the love of her life.

"So you have no need for revenge?" His voice sounded hollow and empty. "No wish to put a stop once and for all to the Grimmox?" This seemed so unlike him, so foreign. Even when they had had differences of opinion in the past, he had always respected her position.

Tears streamed down her face, she felt as though she were on trial. "Why are you questioning me like this? You're starting to sound more and more like Elder Silo...." She jumped to her feet, anger streaking across her face. "Wait, did she put you up to this? Are you interrogating me in this way for her?"

"Answer the question." His eyes grew dark again as though another soul peered out at her. These were not the eyes of Amridon. "You're either with us or against us. Which is it going to be?"

"You sound just like her!" Fury flooded into her face. "I've had enough of this evening." She turned and stormed away.

Amridon shook his head as though he was trying to clear it. "Thula, wait." He rushed after her and put his arm on her shoulder to hold her back.

She spun around, caught off guard by his sudden change. His body seemed filled with emotion, but he looked more like himself—still, there were some things that were just unforgivable. "I'm sorry, I just can't talk to you right now. Coming here on her behalf... it's just unbelievable."

"Wait, what? What happened? We were having a nice dinner. I don't understand." Confusion filled his face. She almost felt bad for him; he looked so small and so lost.

She could tell he had no idea what she was talking about, but she was too upset to deal with it tonight. "I don't know what's going on, or why you're acting this way, but I've had enough. We can discuss it further tomorrow." Trying to hide the frustration littering her face, she turned to leave.

The Final Offering

He ran to catch up to her. "At least let me walk you home," he pleaded.

"No! I'm fine, and I need to sort through my thoughts alone."

As much as it pained her, she walked away leaving him standing in the bright moonlight of the evening, looking dumbfounded. At least he seemed to listen to her request and stayed back, giving her space.

Infuriated, she climbed the stairs leading up several levels of the tree and headed toward her barracks. A shiver up her spine, and sensed someone watching her. She stopped and looked over her shoulder. No one stood behind her and she chalked the uneasy feelings up to the way Amridon had acted. Like a switch, he had seemed to change personalities. What he spoke of and how he spoke it completely reminded her of Silonia.

She trembled as she turned and continued her ascent, walking toward the doors of the barracks, when a sudden urge came over her. For some reason, she decided she didn't want to go in and face the other soldiers. What she needed was time to reflect on everything Amridon had said, how he had acted. Instead, she decided to continue walking, strolling out to the tip of the branch where she could think, alone.

The tiny hairs on her back stood up, and she turned around again. No matter how hard she tried, she couldn't shake the feeling someone followed her, but she still couldn't see anything suspicious. She quieted her breathing and stood still, taking in her surroundings, using every skill she had learned over the past several months. She didn't see anything out of the ordinary but wondered if she should make her way to her room after all.

Deciding it was the best course of action she trusted her instincts and began the walk back the way she had come. If the elders could somehow brainwash Amridon, there was no saying how far they would or wouldn't go.

Nearing the halfway point back to the barracks, she heard rustling from behind her. She turned just in time to see someone in black silk clothing—a cloth covering their face—jump down on her from another branch. Thinking quickly she tried to move, but it was too late. They collided and the weight of her attacker pinned her to the ground. Out of nowhere, a sharp pain ran through her upper arm, stinging like an intense bug bite. She tried her best to fight off her attacker, even landing a kick to his or her groin, but her limbs grew sluggish. Blackness overcame her as her strength diminished.

The Final Offering

Chapter 15

Thula slowly opened her eyes. Several faces stared down at her in a blurry reverie. Her head thumped with pain; every heartbeat ringing one after another like a bell tolling twelve o'clock. She couldn't remember what happened; her body felt weak, and she struggled to even move her head and blink her eyes. The pain made it difficult to focus as she tried to figure out what had happened to her.

"She's awake, she's awake! Amridon, come over here," someone shouted.

She blinked her eyes as she stared up. The vision of her ceiling told her she lay in a bed in her barracks. The dark skin and smooth features of Amridon's face filled her vision.

"Hey there," he said. A tremulous smile crossed his concerned face. "How are you doing?"

She propped herself up on her elbows. "I feel like I've been struck with a rock to my head. What happened?"

"We were hoping you would tell us. Two of your bunkmates stumbled across your unconscious body when they returned from a stroll. They carried you back here, where we've watched over you for most of the evening. The medic inspected you and found what looks like a bug bite on your arm."

The pain persisted as she rubbed her forehead. Slowly her memories returned. "It wasn't a bug bite," she bit her lip in anger. "And I'm still mad at you." She winced as the beating in her head reminded her to be calm.

Anxiety once again creased his face. "Yes, well... I still don't know what I did, but we can worry about that later. I'll do everything I can to make it up to you, but my concern is for you. And what do you mean it wasn't a bug bite?"

Irritation flittered across her face as she thought about their dinner, but she figured he was right. They would work it out later. "After I left you I had this nervous sensation someone was following me. I threw away everything we've learned in our training, and I ignored it." She continued to recount the events of the evening, frustration with herself vying for top spot on her list of reasons and people to blame for her current predicament.

"A person dropped on me and injected something into my arm. The next thing I remember is waking up here with all of you."

The Final Offering

The frown on Amridon's forehead furrowed deeper. "Who would've attacked you? I don't understand."

"Whoever it was wore all black and had a piece of cloth wrapped around their face so I couldn't see who it was."

Amridon slammed his fist into the palm of his other hand. "It had to be a Grimmox! Who else could it have been?"

"I don't know that I would jump down that rabbit hole just yet. There is no reason to think it was the Grimmox," she said.

"What do you mean? No Haloti would ever do this to one of their own." Thula watched as disgust quickly chased the anger across his face.

She thought differently, and if news spread of her attack, it would only add more fodder to the cannon. This was exactly what the elders needed to justify their new programs. If her suspicions were correct, Silonia was behind the attack, but to say that to Amridon would only cause her more problems, especially after what happened earlier.

"Explain to me how a Grimmox would get so far into our territory undetected?" she asked.

"They're sneaky, conniving creatures. This is exactly why I joined the program. It's time to put a stop to them before they carry out whatever devious acts they have planned," he said with a vehemence she was beginning to abhor.

Getting nowhere fast, she shook her head in disgust. Amridon seemed too far gone. After weeks of Silonia's propaganda-filled lectures, what more should she expect? "I'm sure there will be an investigation. Let's just wait and see what comes of it before we jump to any conclusions."

Amridon harrumphed. "Investigation? Why do we need to wait for an investigation? The way I see it, there can only be one conclusion." He looked around in an attempt to garner support from the others gathered around her bed.

"Yes well, you're probably right." She sighed, bringing her hand up and rubbing her forehead. "You know, I'm pretty tired and I have a splitting headache. I appreciate all of your concern," she looked at everyone gathered around her. "I need to rest. After all, we have training tomorrow." She managed a shaky smile.

She received many words of encouragement from several soldiers in her unit as they left her in peace. Much to her dismay, Amridon remained behind.

"I'm sorry I offended you this evening. Worse than anything, it's horrible I wasn't around to protect you when I should have been." He smiled reassuringly. "If you will just tell me how to fix this, I would do it in a heartbeat. You're the most important person in my life."

You have a funny way of showing it, she thought and smiled softly. "I'm not ready to reconcile just yet. Give me time, and when I'm ready, I promise you I'll give you the opportunity to repair this damage. If you don't mind, I need to rest."

He tried to speak, but she laid back and closed her eyes. In defeat, he sighed and turned. She opened her eyes a crack and watched him walk away, suddenly feeling very uncomfortable with her decision to join the program. Every instinct told her to walk up to the commander and quit, to just run away and put all

The Final Offering

of her troubles behind her. But, she had a suspicion this would only make matters worse for her.

She lay in bed and pretended to sleep as her head continued to throb. Each heartbeat was like a nail thrust into her brain, and it was hard not to cry. After several hours of tossing and turning, she decided to get out of bed shortly before sunup.

She needed fresh air, so she walked out into the crisp morning; dew covered the tree branch and delicately dripped from the sharp edges of the green leaves. As she left the barracks, she spotted several guards, a new addition to their current numbers. Had they been there last night, there probably wouldn't have been an attack.

"Thula, we've been asked to bring you before the commander. If you would please follow us?" one of them asked.

She hesitantly followed the officers as they turned and walked away. *What now?* She thought as she looked at the horizon and saw the first orange rays gently kissing the rolling hills to the east. The unknown seemed to follow her and she couldn't help her anxiousness about what was about to happen.

They escorted her into the commander's office in their practiced, stiff shuffle. He sat at a desk, surrounded by four other officers, and she wasn't surprised in the least to see Silonia standing behind him.

At her arrival, the commander stood and smiled. "Thula, what a pleasure to meet you." A concerned look crossed his dark face. "I only wish it were under better circumstances."

Thula noticed Silonia eagerly watching her reaction under her thick, bushy eyebrows. Thula nodded. She didn't quite know how to respond but figured she needed to guard her tongue.

"Please, Thula, take a seat." The commander motioned toward an empty chair.

She did as instructed and sat uncomfortably in the chair under the watchful glare of the officers and the elder. An unevenness flowed through her, their eyes following her and giving the impression they tried to peer into her soul.

The commander shoved a couple pieces of paper aside before he spoke. "We understand you were attacked last night. Are you doing okay? Did you sustain any serious injuries?"

"Yes, I was." She decided to keep her voice as unstilted as possible by keeping her answers short. They wouldn't read anything of her true feelings if she kept out all emotion. "I was checked out by the doctor and he says I should be fine physically."

The commander smiled. "That is good news. Did you happen to get a look at who did this?" he asked.

"Unfortunately, I didn't see who it was. They had their face covered by a piece of cloth."

"As I suspected. Well... I just want you to hear that Elder Silonia suggested we station troops to stand guard around our region. If anyone else tries something similar, we'll be ready for them. We want all of our citizens to be protected and make sure nothing like this ever happens again. Which is why, with Silonia's blessing, we've stationed soldiers around all of our territories. We wanted you to be the first to know."

The Final Offering

She offered a fake smile, hoping it was enough to satisfy the commander. Silonia wore a smug look of satisfaction. "I'm glad to hear of such precautions. Do you have enough troops to man all the new assignments?" She didn't care. Could care less, to be exact, but she wanted to appear engaged—and if truth be told, she wanted information.

The commander smiled broadly. "The elders are continuing with the postponement of the tattoo placement. We're now accepting volunteers, and after news spread of your attack last night, young Haloti are signing up for service in record numbers. If this keeps up, over fifty percent of our youth will be in the service of the military."

Thula looked at Silonia out of the corner of her eye. Hidden beneath the rough exterior of the elder's face, she could sense grim satisfaction. Everything was going her way, and if it kept up, there would be little the rest of the Haloti could do to stand in the way of the council.

"You all must be excited, and I have to admit I feel much safer," she lied. "I guess the barracks will soon fill up with new recruits."

"Very soon indeed. We might even need to build more." He grinned. "Not to belittle your anguish from last night's events, but I guess we have you to thank for all of this."

A sharp pain, like that of a knife plunging repeatedly into her midsection filled her stomach, and a lump closed her throat. *This is all because of me*, she thought. *How could I have been so stupid?*

"Thank you for telling me, sir, and I appreciate all the precautions." She offered a warm smile. "Is there anything else you need of me? I'm still recovering from the attack, and I also need to try to put food in my stomach before training begins today."

The commander seemed taken aback. "Yes... well, I understand, but you won't be participating in any of today's events. It would be best if you took a day for yourself."

She bit her lip; thick, blood slowly filled her mouth. "I thank you for your concern, but I'm well enough to take part fully today."

The commander stood up, and Silonia spoke into his ear. "I'm afraid protocol mandates you take at least the next day off. I understand you're excelling in the program and fear falling behind, but there is no need to be apprehensive about it. You won't miss much." His smile did nothing to remove any of her concerns.

"I don't see the point." She sighed. "But if it is your command, then I will follow." She stood to leave.

The commander made it a point to walk around his desk. "Thank you for all you've done and I wish you a speedy recovery," he said as he ushered her out of the room.

She couldn't tell if his words were sincere, or if he knew as much as Silonia and was just doing all of this for show. The words sounded genuine, but she left the meeting with entirely different thoughts coursing through her mind than she had had when they summoned her. It was crazy how one little decision could change and affect so many things. She couldn't shake the dread that she might now be used as a puppet, a sort of deceitful advertising ploy to usher in more support for the elders.

The Final Offering

Everything seemed to slip through her fingers like tiny grains of sand. She didn't know what she had gotten herself into, and the more she learned, the more fleeting everything she thought seemed to become. With few other choices, she would have to fall in line now and do what everyone expected of her. Until she was ready to make her move that was.

The Final Offering

Chapter 16

Thula cracked open her eyes and smiled as she listened to the beautiful song of a male mountain bluebird as it attempted to woo its mate. There was no better way to wake up as the sun crested the horizon marking the sign of dawn. After wiping the sleep from her eyes, she stretched in her bed, enjoying the moment, until she remembered where she was.

With a satisfied smile on her face, she looked around the barracks as the bright early rays spread across the room like hungry tendrils eagerly searching the wooden floor for anything to grab onto and devour. The smile quickly fell when she spotted her silk dress uniform she had laid out the evening before.

The past several months had been a mixed bag, and she was glad her training had come to an end, but now her entire unit would be a tool the elders could use at their disposal. They had even moved the completion ceremony into the city square of the village so they could make it a public spectacle and show everyone how well the program had worked and hopefully garner added support.

The elders were anything but dumb. Others out there doubted everything they were doing. People just like her who understood there was an underlying threat that maybe it wasn't the Grimmox after all. What better way for the council to prove to the naysayers their cause was a just one by trotting out one of their own—one who not only agreed with them on all fronts and completed the program but someone who had fallen victim to a ruthless attack as well.

Yes, she hated this and figured she was about to become the poster child of the elders. *Just a couple more days*, she told herself. *A couple more days and I will have my post. Then I can find out what is really happening, and bring proof back and show the world what's been going on.*

Her feet hit the cold, wooden floor of her barracks and she sighed. The ceremony wouldn't start until later in the day, so she went for a run. The temperature had already dropped and the normally vibrant, green leaves were reddening on the edges. Soon the leaves would transform to their yellow, orange, or red color, before creating a soft blanket covering the thick, green grass of the ground below.

She stepped out into the fresh morning air, already heavy with moisture. The full sun crested the horizon as she ran with no destination in mind. Several hummingbirds flew near her.

The Final Offering

They floated in the air, watching her every movement. They both darted away when she fluttered her wings in response. She smiled at the simplicity of the birds.

Lost in her thoughts, she ran and ran as the sun drew ever higher in the sky. It was almost as if she were hypnotized with thought for nothing else, when an angry chipmunk on the nearby cedar tree, yelling at a large dog in the prairie, snapped her out of her trance. She shook her head to return to a normal line of thinking and looked at the sky. The day had slipped away from her. The start of the ceremony would soon be on her, which left her with little time to prepare. *I need to grab something to eat before I get ready. Who knows long it will be before dinner...* She freshened up and hastily donned her clothing, finishing in enough time to join several other members of her unit as they made their way down to the village.

The others tried to engage her in conversation, but her head wasn't in it—for a number of reasons. She was polite, but she thought she spied a couple of them adopting looks of concern. Over the past several weeks, she had done everything in her power to toe the line. But she used the opportunity to gather information, which she hoped to give to her sister after the commencement ceremony. They would get the weekend off before receiving their first deployment orders. The thought of being in the company of people who held the same views she did was refreshing and gave her something to look forward to.

After what seemed like an eternity, they made it to the village square. As she had expected, it looked like the entire village had turned up for the ceremony. She had no idea what the elders had in store, but she prepared herself for a bout of propaganda. A quick glance at the assembled soldier, and she found her position in the formation—an easy task given she ranked above most of the others—positioned up front. This also made it convenient for Silonia to point her out to several other elders in attendance. Awaiting the ceremony, she stood uneasily at attention. Amridon was at her side, as unit commander, but lately, she had drawn no comfort from his company.

The heat from the sun increased and beads of sweat formed on her brow as she waited. She wanted to brush it away but had trained to ignore it, and to do otherwise would show weakness, especially considering who was in attendance. Finally, the commander walked forward.

The governor made a quick, irrelevant speech and introduced the commander. "I would like to start by saying hello to the friends and families of the fine class of soldiers assembled before us. This is a new program, and as such, we had to create a new training regimen. I'm happy to say everyone in attendance today has done an exemplary job throughout the past several months…"

He continued to speak on, but Thula had no wish to listen to the useless drivel. Using only her peripheral vision, she scanned the audience. Her mother and father sat next to each other near the front row. His arms were wrapped lovingly around her waist as they listened intently to the commander. She couldn't blame them. It wasn't every day their daughter completed a course with honors. They were proud of her and she assumed she would be too if the situation were reversed.

Her sister, Tilfin, with the other devoted Haloti. It almost appeared as though her sister were praying; her lips moved ever so slightly in a rhythmic manner. It didn't bother her that her sister was so devout, but she didn't know how deep in her sister

The Final Offering

was, and didn't think she could trust her, not with the details anyway.

Using the edge of her vision, she continued to scan the crowd. Trana sat with a group of schoolchildren and the image brought a smile to her face. There was something comforting in the care her sister had for the children, amused as her sister pointed to the commander, the rows of soldiers; taking the time to speak to each child individually. *Always teaching,* Thula thought. She wondered how hard it was for her sister to teach something she didn't believe herself. How frustrating it must be. Then again, was she not in a similar predicament? Graduating from a program that at its core was against everything she held dear. It was so frustrating, even humiliating at times.

Her eyes drifted outside of the crowd, and she spotted a large number of soldiers in attendance—normally not an oddity considering the program they were about to witness—armed and on watch. They were spaced evenly around the entire gathering of people, eyes on constant alert for any danger. She felt trapped, as though they were being held captive, not protected. Just a village of loyal citizens....

"Thula! Is everything okay?" the commander asked her. She snapped out of her thoughts and realized the address.

Amridon wore a slight smirk. "They've called your name three times. Are you okay?" he asked in a hushed whisper.

"Yes, Commander," she said.

Looking a little embarrassed, the commander spoke. "I asked if you would join me at the podium, please."

All eyes—and not just those of her unit or the assembled officers and elders on the dais—were on her as she broke out of formation and marched to the front. Once there she saluted the officers.

He spoke softly to her. "Please turn and face the audience. As I was stating before, Thula completed the program at the head of her class. As a reward for all of her hard work, and in recognition of her skills, she is promoted from this day forward to sergeant."

Applause rang out through the crowd. She blushed as the commander pinned an insignia on the breast of her shirt. Her eyes scanned the crowd as the commander's hot breath prickled the hairs on her neck. There was no missing the pride in her father's eyes, and the reproach in her sister Trana's. They would definitely have to have a conversation later.

The commander saluted her, and she returned it before he spoke again. "It has never been reported before—we withheld her name so her family wouldn't worry—but a couple of short weeks ago, Thula was attacked as she returned home from a private dinner."

A hush and several murmurs spread through the crowd as they understood and put a face to the story they had heard rumored; the story, which had warranted the changes in procedures enacted throughout all of their territory.

Thula shifted uncomfortably in front of the audience. Just as she had anticipated, she was being used as propaganda. From this day forward, she would now be the face of the Haloti resistance and she hated herself for it.

The Final Offering

"We've investigated the incident and unfortunately turned up no leads. No real physical harm befell her, but whatever happened caused young Thula here to blackout. Her assailant wore a piece of silk on their face to conceal it, and she never got a good look at them."

The crowd sat silently in anticipation. Somebody had to pay for attacking an innocent young woman, and they all wanted to hear more of what was in store.

"If I had to wager a guess, I would assume it was the Grimmox." Angry voices filled the crowd, seemingly from both those who agreed and disagreed with him. "As a result, we have placed guards in all of our cities and have increased patrols. From the graciousness of the governor and the council of elders, we have a dire need for added troops. As we indicated before, our traditions have been placed on hold and we are looking for more citizens to join the cause. Sign-up sheets will be available following today's ceremony for any who may be interested in joining."

As if on cue, and just like the first sighting of the Grimmox, several officers brought out temporary tables and sat down with large stacks of paperwork.

"We want all of our fine citizens to know they can walk the branches at night safe and secure. This has necessitated the increased patrols, but it is all to preserve our way of life. With your help," he pointed to the audience, "we will continue to preserve our customs, and we'll take the fight to the home of the Grimmox." Cheers erupted from the crowd. Thula was displeased by the number who may have been swayed in such a short period.

The commander dismissed her before continuing with the ceremony. Thula walked back to her position with her head held down in shame. She should present herself in a better light with better posture and an air of confidence, but it was lost on her. The humiliation was too much and she could almost feel the elders' eyes piercing her back like daggers.

Regaining her composure, she stood at attention while the ceremony droned on. She couldn't listen; she had no wish to do so. Every fiber of her being wanted the whole thing to be over with so she could retreat to her parents' home—her sanctuary.

She had no idea how much time had passed when she noticed several soldiers in her unit cheer and relax. Looking around with dazed eyes, many embraced one another in congratulatory hugs. Several grabbed her and offered her their blessings and excitement for her new position. She thanked them and disappeared as quickly as she could.

Scanning the audience, she found her parents and joined their sides. What had been large, beaming smiles disappeared as they noticed her morose demeanor.

Her mother was the first to speak. "Thula, what's wrong?"

She shook her head and tried to keep the questions away.

"What's wrong?" her father asked. "We're so proud of you and all you have accomplished. Why do you look so sad? Was it the attack? We're glad you're okay. We didn't realize anything had even happened."

Tears welling up in the corners of her eyes. "Can we go home?" she asked. "I can't stand it here."

The Final Offering

"Certainly! Stay close," her father said. He held her close, and her mother moved in on the other side. They hastily moved through the crowd, pulling her away from many who wanted to talk to her. They were greeted by puzzled looks and much concern but most assumed she must be exhausted, and they cleared a path for her and her parents as they weaved through the mob.

The Final Offering

Chapter 17

They arrived back at their home and guided Thula to a couch in the main room. Her tears streamed down her face and she sobbed into her father's shoulder. Cellomes grabbed a piece of cloth and wiped the wetness away from her daughter's face. "There, there, everything will be all right."

Thula looked up into her mother and father's faces, "No! No, it's not," she said in a hushed voice as her face flushed with anger. "Nothing will be all right ever again, at least not for me."

"Why don't you explain what happened. Help us understand why you're so upset." Her father spoke with sincerity in his voice.

"I don't know where to begin." Her father offered a look urging her to go ahead. "You both know why I joined the program. I wanted to be with Amridon, but more importantly…"

The door to her family's home flew open and Trana came rushing into the house. "What the heck was all of that? I thought we were on the same side." She paused while taking in the scene. "Why are you crying?"

Thula stood and ran over to her sister. "It's been horrible, Trana."

Trana embraced Thula and lightly stroked her hair. "Shh shh shh, it's okay." She looked confused. "Can you tell me about it?"

Thula sobbed again. In an effort to calm herself, she sat back down. "I've been so foolish. I thought I could be careful, that no one would see what I was doing." Her father looked nervous by her statement. "There was an elder conducting part of our training. And I thought I had been so sly, but she saw right through me."

Her mother rubbed her leg to soothe her. "Are you in any trouble? I mean, should we be worried?"

"She summoned me to her quarters several weeks ago and questioned my motives. It seems she couldn't understand why I looked so disinterested and unmoved by her teachings."

Thula recounted everything, leaving nothing out as her family sat back in shock.

"And I know it was them. They're trying to pin it on the Grimmox, but why would a Grimmox assailant attack me with their face concealed? It was dark, but his—and it was a man, they were too strong for a woman—skin was dark like my own. I could see little, but I swear the skin was dark."

They all sat in silence for several moments. Finally, her father spoke. "Why would they attack one of their own and pin it on someone else?"

Thula sat forward on the edge of her seat. "Don't you see? That's the beauty of the whole thing. Look what has happened in the aftermath. Guards are stationed everywhere. They're signing up more new recruits. This is what they wanted; they now have a reason to build up the military, and I can only assume it is a cover so someday soon we can go on the offensive against the Grimmox." She stared at the wall. "I fell right into their trap. The worst part is I'm a tool they can use to support their purposes. I 'm disgusted and a little dirty."

"There is nothing you can do about that, honey. You had no idea any of this would happen," her mother said.

"Yes, but that's just it. I should have been ready for something like this. After all, didn't I join up because I was suspicious? I should have been on higher alert."

They tried to soothe and comfort her. Eventually, they ate dinner and spoke of happier things to get her mind off the pain and misery she experienced. It wasn't lost on Thula her sister had remained quiet throughout dinner. She wondered what her sister's thoughts were.

Shortly after dinner, her parents retired to their own room leaving Trana and Thula alone on the couch. "I'm truly sorry for the trials you've faced. I really thought it would be no issue."

She smiled at her sister, pleased she wanted to discuss it further. "I didn't think it would be either. Then again, I'm young and naïve. I should've known better."

Trana's body inched closer to Thula's as her eagerness showed through. "Not to diminish the feelings you're having, but have you learned anything?"

"Just what I've told you. If my hunches are correct, though, I don't think the Grimmox ever even ventured into our territory at all. They have and will continue to use our fear against us, knowing with the right words they can get anything they want. It all just depends on how they present it." She paused as her sister nodded in agreement. "And then I dropped a gift right into their lap. I'm the perfect scapegoat, and I single-handedly gave them the opportunity to put their plans into action."

"Do you think it's only the elders? Or are the high-ranking officers in on it too?" Trana asked.

"I've had a lot of time to reflect on that very question. I wondered myself, but the more I contemplate it, the more I realize this is all the work of the elders. We are all puppets who move around satisfying each one of their whims."

"What comes next? Do you anticipate any further danger?"

Anger crossed Thula's face; her cheeks turned red. "After this weekend I will have a post. Considering I now have a higher rank, I doubt I will have a menial job, and will instead coordinate several of the lower ranking troops. It won't matter though. I will do everything in my power to find evidence. Evidence I can use against the council, to show the rest of the world how they pull all the strings. That none of this was anything more than a large thrust for power. From what I can tell, the council won't rest until they have taken control of the entire tree." She stared at her sister with stern eyes. "I've made it my duty to make sure it never happens, even if it means sacrificing my life."

"That surely isn't naïve or young sounding. I'm proud of you. Let me know if there is anything I can do to help." Trana hugged her sister. "And Thula, please be careful."

"I will," she lied. Many thoughts ran through her mind, but being careful wasn't one of them. As the day progressed, her pain and sadness transformed into anger and motivation. She took all it and stuffed it in her gut. As the moments ticked by, she stewed and grew angrier. It wasn't ideal, but she was holding back for the right opportunity to explode, and she had a bad feeling the explosion would come sooner, rather than later.

The Final Offering

Chapter 18

After a long and emotional weekend, she arrived back at the barracks where she received her command. As she suspected, eight troops from the unit were put under her direct command, and they were directed to a post on the northwest side of the tree. Their orders were to keep a watch while sending two soldiers at a time further down below into Grimmox territory. From there, they would start scouting missions to see what they could learn. The missions would last sixteen hours each day, and the soldiers would rotate at regular intervals. Of course, they ordered her not to engage in the scouting missions but instead asked her to coordinate the communications back to headquarters.

Eight soldiers stood before her as she looked them over to decide their strengths. They were a mixed bag, really. A couple had done well, and she gave each of them a weaker soldier to go with them on the missions, hoping their aptitude would make up for any the others lacked. The last thing she wanted was to fail in her first command. She suspected they monitored her and didn't want to give any more fuel for the elders' fires.

They set out at mid-morning and made the hike to their post, selecting a large, flat branch that would serve as their home for the next several weeks. The area was well concealed, and although they were still in *Haloti* territory, she still wanted to be careful. She saw a stubby branch just to the south of their new base. It was positioned a couple of paces higher in the tree shrouded in leaves. It would be the perfect spot for her to run her operations, and carry out her own spying missions. With her spyglass, she thought it would give the ideal perch to gather all the evidence she would need. Of course, before too long, the leaves would fall and there would be no place to hide. She had to take advantage by getting the information she so dearly sought.

After everyone settled and made arrangements for sleeping, she paired each of the soldiers, based on the abilities she had seen over the past several months. She then assigned each pair a number, telling them they would each take an eight-hour shift, which they would split in half. For four hours, they would conduct their scouting, and for the other four, they would cover the other pair as they conducted their mission. That way each pair had a backup that could move in quickly if they encountered any enemies. She would stay in her perch for sixteen hours each day because she didn't want to miss a thing.

The Final Offering

Wanting to keep them fresh, she gave the remaining sixteen hours for them to do as they pleased, but she suggested they try to rest for at least a couple hours during the day. They would have to post watches at night and she wanted each of them to be rested when their eight-hour shift began. Communication was an important part of their mission and would require that one of them run back for her, but she anticipated this would be few and far between as she didn't really expect any action.

Considering their late start to the day, today's shifts would only be four hours for each pair, with two conducting missions and two on watch. She sent off the first four and ordered one pair to report back to the commander they had arrived and begun their mission. She climbed up the thick, cracking bark and nestled herself into her perch. Digging in her pack, she pulled out her spyglass and brought it up to her eye. The first pair expertly positioned themselves well within Grimmox territory. Her heart beat hard in her chest as she looked on in anticipation. She didn't expect anything to happen, but she was still responsible for each of the young soldiers, and this wasn't something she took lightly.

Eventually, her heart slowed, and she observed with a calm demeanor. Scanning each of the branches, she was careful to keep her spyglass out of the direct rays of light. The last thing she needed was to give away their position by an unintended reflection.

She pulled out an empty journal, a feather, and her inkpot and readied herself to take notes. Continuing to watch, she wasn't surprised when the afternoon drew on and everything remained relatively peaceful.

J.G. Gatewood

The first pair finished their first rotation as she grew bored. They switched positions with the other pair, just as the two soldiers returned from HQ and told her they had relayed the message. No further orders were issued, and she released the two so they could enjoy the next two hours before it was their turn. She smiled when they walked over to their beds, and quickly fell asleep. It was a hot afternoon, but their quick trip to command—it was quick as she hadn't expected them back for at least another hour—seemed to have sapped all of their strength. One of them snored loud enough to shake the smaller limbs of the tree, and she couldn't help herself and she chuckled.

The new pair moved into position and she watched their movements through her spyglass. She was pleased; this pair had taken what they observed the first set do and learned from it. They ventured farther into the Grimmox territory and she realized she would have to give them better guidelines going forward. They ventured too far away from their backup and it could have potentially dangerous consequences if she didn't discuss it. Luckily, the first pair noticed and followed them farther down the branch. A commotion arose to the south, and she held her breath in anticipation, but her fear quickly subsided when two birds flew out and squabbled in the air.

The rest of the afternoon moved along without any newsworthy events. As the sun neared the mountains in the west—ready to nuzzle down behind them for the evening—she found herself disappointed because they hadn't sited a Grimmox. She didn't know what she had expected, but she had hoped to see one. Whether they were behind this or not, they were still creatures she had heard about her entire life and she was eager to lay her eyes upon one.

The Final Offering

She climbed down from her perch; her stomach a grumbling knot in her midsection, and rejoined the others for the evening. One of the soldiers had started a fire in a clay pot, and the others sat around it, all at work preparing dinner.

"I would just like to commend each one of you for a job well done today." She looked at the second pair. "I would remind you, though, we will be at this for the next several weeks. Garma, Villani, you both seemed eager for your first mission and traveled farther than acceptable. Be glad Mithal and Quento both had your backs and followed you to make sure you were covered." She smiled at them to lighten the admonishment. "We're all eager and ready to prove ourselves. I feel the same way but let's try to take it a little slower. At least until we have eyes on the Grimmox and better understand their routines."

The young soldiers nodded their agreement. Quinto ladled vegetables in a meat gravy onto each of their plates, and they all sat back and relaxed for the evening. It was their first night out in the wilderness, away from the comforts of their homes—even the stoic accommodations of the barracks—and just the thought of being so close to enemy territory had them each on edge.

She decided to lift the mood and invited each of the soldiers to share some of their past with the others. It would be good if they each knew more about their compatriots and hoped it would help to put their minds more at ease.

After the last soldier, Garma finished her tale, Thula yawned and stretched her back. Sleep was ready to take over her and she needed to rest. Using the same number as before, she set the watch with each pair covering two hours. The last two hours she would take for herself. Given her rank, it wasn't necessary, but she wanted to show them she wouldn't order them to do anything she wouldn't do herself.

After she gathered several leaves, she laid down beneath the thick blankets she had brought from home. She stared into the black abyss of the sky, the stars danced and sparkled before her eyes. It felt hypnotic, and she found a trancelike state. In her mind, she thanked her parents for all they had taught her and prayed to Halothias for protection to last through their first night and through her first command.

It wasn't long before she drifted off to sleep, dreaming about the Grimmox—although she had never seen one, her brain seemed to have an idea of what one looked like. There was no tossing or turning. For the first time in a long time, she slept peacefully—for a couple of hours, anyway.

The branch swung frantically in the wind and she sat upright. A large breeze blew from the west. Raindrops fell from the sky in rapid succession. Thunder boomed through the air as the icy tendrils of lightning crawled through the black night sky. White light filled the sky in a flash as she jumped to her feet. In the momentary blinding, white light, she thought she saw a face. Of course, she assumed she must have imagined it, but she stared, waiting for the next flash of lightning.

When it came, she saw the face again. She tried to recreate the picture in her mind and gasped. It reminded her of Silonia, which frightened her. At the next flash, she thought the face was close to her as if floating in midair, then even closer and she wanted to crawl out of her skin. She took a step back, followed by another, and then another. Soon she had backed herself up against the thick trunk of the tree. Her first instincts were to fight, that was what she was trained for after all, but panic

The Final Offering

gripped her and she found herself paralyzed by fear. Trapped and helpless, the face came closer and closer, mocking her and laughing at her fear. When the face was on top of her, she shut her eyes and cringed, trembling as she searched for some shelter in the tree. If she could only get inside, she would be safe.

Even through the biting chill of the wind, hot breath tickled her face and neck. It sent a shiver down her spine. She thought she heard laughter and every cell in her body screamed to get away. Waiting for something deadly to attack her, she pinched her eyes shut even further. Petrified, she forgot all about her training and felt like a little girl trapped by a bully. As sudden, as it had come on, it was gone. The breathing, the laughter, all of it gone. She opened her eyes and stared out. The storm persisted, but whatever she saw in the flashes of light had disappeared. Her heart calmed as relief flooded her.

Her soldiers were all awake too, and they stared at her in disbelief. Concern filled their faces as they stood back and watched.

"It's all right. I had a bad dream." She cringed inwardly at what they must have just seen their sergeant do in the throes of a nightmare.

Garma rushed over to her side. "Is there anything I can do? Do you need anything?"

"I appreciate your concern and your offer, but I will be fine now." She sighed as she looked at the others. "If you can, go back to sleep. I'll take the rest of the night."

There were protests at her words.

"You'll be exhausted tomorrow."

"We really don't mind sharing the watch."

"Thank you, but I doubt I will sleep any more tonight. Maybe one of you can take mine tomorrow night to make up for it." She smiled at them.

There were several offers and her smile persisted. One day as their commander and they already seemed respectful of her position. It warmed her heart.

One by one, they drifted off to sleep. When she was sure they were all out for the night, she made her way up to her new perch. Pulling out her spyglass, she took a deep breath to get herself back on track. She scanned the surrounding areas, not that she could see much, but she did it anyway.

The Final Offering

Chapter 19

After three weeks at their post, everyone had had enough. So far, they hadn't spotted a single Grimmox, to be specific they hadn't spotted *anything* at all. With only two days remaining before they needed to return to the village, they all felt worthless. The leaves all changed color now and barely clung to their branches in a last-ditch effort. Soon they wouldn't hold on any longer and would fall to the ground. This meant the offering was approaching. She hadn't even thought about it in months. She'd been too busy to worry about such a thing, and she found she no longer cared.

She watched as Mithal and Quento moved into position, venturing farther than ever before, and Thula instructed the third pair to join in as a backup. With no idea why she had a strong inkling something would happen. Her training taught her to follow her instincts, and it hadn't let her down yet.

With their lack of success, she wondered why they had undergone so much training and prep work. It seemed one of two things was going on. Either she was right, and the Grimmox were no threat, minding the boundaries, staying well within their own territory, or Silonia sent her to an area devoid of any Grimmox activity.

Her soldiers trained for more than they now faced; it wasn't fair for them to be punished because the elder didn't trust her. She sighed as she raised the spyglass to her eye. Mithal shrank to the branch and sought the cover of the orange leaves. She moved the glass and saw the rest of the soldiers followed suit and disappeared. *Man, they're good*, she thought. A quick flash of pride lashed through her.

A black caterpillar with yellow stripes meandered its way out onto their branch. It moved slowly, but deliberately, its movement reminiscent of a wave as it inched forward. She heard the slightest rustle and moved the glass in its direction. Her mouth fell open, and she shoved her hand in front of it to stifle her gasp. A shiver ran up her back and the hairs there extended.

Two figures climbed the trunk, both males with light skin. One had shorter blond hair, and the other long dark hair shaved bare to the skin on the sides of his head. They both had muscular bodies, which she could see as they wore leather breaches, but no shirts, with opaque wings adorning their backs. They looked to be a little taller than her, with bigger ears. The thing that mesmerized her the most were their tattoos. Since their skin was so much lighter, the colors were vibrant. They

The Final Offering

twisted up the sides of their bodies and up their neck, like a vine's crawling tendrils finding space anywhere it can. She could see traces of the tattoo on the shaved skin where the one had cut his hair. The reds, blues, and greens stood out magnificently.

In awe, she watched for several moments before clearing her head. She pulled the glass to her eye and took a closer look. Her vision moved up one of them from his feet, to his torso, and up to his head. Having heard stories of monsters who preyed on the Haloti her whole life, she didn't know what she expected. But these, they looked like her own people. These weren't monsters; if anything, they could be distant brothers.

They both had their bows drawn and stalked the creature. In unison, as if their minds were connected, they let their arrows fly. The *throng* of the strings filled the air as the arrows whistled toward their target. She watched on in admiration and somehow missed them reloading. Before she realized it, two more arrows were in the air. All four found their target within inches of one another, and the caterpillar slumped to the branch, uttering its last cry, before falling dead.

Remembering her troops, she looked at their hiding spots with haste. So far, they seemed relaxed, content to sit back and watch the Grimmox. She only hoped they realized how long they would be stuck in their current positions. The task of skinning and cleaning a caterpillar of this size was arduous. They were in for a long afternoon, and judging by the Grimmox's skill with the bow, she hoped they could stay hidden and not draw any attention to themselves.

They expertly skinned the creature and cut into the flesh. She even learned a few techniques she decided she would try them when she returned home. The sun moved through the sky as they dismantled the carcass. What should have taken them half the day to carry out, they pulled off in just a couple hours.

The furry skin was still drying in what little heat the sun provided today. As they waited, they wrapped the meat in leaves making transportable bundles. They filled up their arms—taking only a fraction of the meat, but as much as they could carry at once—and headed out, using their wings as they jumped down several branches.

This was their chance. She whistled and saw movement from all three pairs. She waved her arms, urging them all to return. Presumably, they too realized they only had a couple moments and made their way back to their own territory.

She climbed down from her perch and joined up with her soldiers. They made their way to another branch, well out of the view of Grimmox territory.

With a grin filling his face, Villani said, "Can you believe it? After so many days of nothing, I thought we had no hope of spotting one." He ran his hands through his dark hair. "To think, just two days before we leave and two of them. It's as though Halothias has offered us his blessing and provided for us with this gift."

"What are your orders, sergeant? They will be back within moments," Mithal said. "If we're going to do something, we need to come up with a plan now."

She could see the eagerness on all of their faces. "No. Our orders are to watch. To gather information, and that is exactly what we're going to do."

The Final Offering

Quento tried to protest. "But this has been handed to us. We can move on them before they have any idea we're here."

"I won't start a war just because we're all eager. Do you understand me?" She looked at each of them. "We have our orders, and I expect each of you to follow them."

"But they're Grimmox." Quento pleaded. "Don't you want your revenge? They attacked you and now you have a chance to do the same." Thula could see the debate was getting away from her.

"We could disguise ourselves with cloth around our heads, just like they did to you," Garma said.

Thula grew frustrated. "Enough!" She shouted. "We are only to observe and report and that is what we're going to do. If any of you have an objection to my orders, you can take it up with the officers." A smile filled her face. "Hell, you could even take it up with Silonia. But an order is an order and I expect you all to listen. We will find cover on our branch and we'll *observe*."

It seemed she finally got through to them. At least they seemed to understand she wouldn't sway in her decision.

They made their way back to their branch. The Grimmox seemed busy collecting another load. After waiting for them to jump down, she climbed up to her perch. She placed the others in well-hidden areas where they could see below and observe. Will all her hope, she trusted they would follow her orders.

Back in the safety of her perch, she pulled out her journal. She dabbed the feather in her inkpot and grabbed the spyglass, ready to record the two Grimmox's every movement. It took them several more trips, but they collected all the meat. Although she had a pen in her hand, she found she had nothing to write about—all they were doing was carrying meat—but that all changed when they returned to grab the furry skin.

The blonde-haired Grimmox rubbed his hands in a pool of collected blood. He wiped a streak down his forehead and over his nose. The dark-haired Grimmox did the same. With their faces painted, they dropped to their knees and bowed their heads. They each placed their right arm on the carcass, and their wings folded back, almost solemnly.

Pulling the glass closer, she noticed their lips moving. *What are they doing?* She thought. And then she made the connection; they were praying. She had never seen anything like it before. The Haloti cared for all creatures around them, and knew taking a life to feed themselves was all a part of the cycle of life, but never had she thought about praying over the lifeless hulk, thanking it for what it provided. It was a reverent moment, and she choked back the tears forming in her eyes and the lump welling up in her throat.

After a long period of prayer—and the silence that ensued following it—they stood. They looked out over the branch and surveyed the land stretched out before them. They kissed the pointer and ring finger of their right hand and raised them to the sky in a sort of salute, before turning and collecting the fur.

Thula wasn't certain, but she thought she glimpsed the dark-haired Grimmox's eyes drift up in her direction. He didn't turn and look, but rather seemed to look at her from the corner of his eye. A small smirk appeared at the corner of his mouth. *They know we're watching them,* she thought. *But how can that*

The Final Offering

be? They showed no sign as they stalked, killed, and cleaned the creature.

She was stunned. All along the Grimmox were aware of the Haloti presence. *What was all of this today then?* She asked herself. *Was it just for show?* Figuring she would never have the answers to these questions, but it didn't stop her mind from reeling with thoughts.

They took the skin and jumped off the branch, disappearing below, out of the Haloti soldier's visual range. Once they were gone, she exhaled loudly. She hadn't realized, but she held her breath. Climbing down the tree, she rejoined the others who all clustered together, whispering.

She was glad they finally had some action—that they had seen a Grimmox—but now she had more questions than she did before their appearance. One thing she knew for sure; these were not the monsters they had been made out to be.

The Final Offering

Part II – The Offering

Chapter 1

The two remaining days of their deployment passed with no further sightings of the Grimmox, and Thula was flummoxed. She had hoped they would return so she could gather more information. And truth be told, she was so curious to find out more about them it was all she could think about, but ultimately the days had been uneventful.

She took the rear as her eight soldiers led the way back to the barracks. The mood was heavy and thick. It seemed as though several of the soldiers under her command were disappointed they were given an opportunity to take action against their enemy, but she had ordered them back. She wasn't sure, but she thought she saw resentment from a few.

Ultimately, though, she had made the right decision. Against her better judgment, she followed her orders to the letter, even though she suspected she was never supposed to see a Grimmox in the first place. In the end, the soldiers were young and they would see her point one day.

They reached the barracks by mid-morning, and she released them. They had the week off for the offering. Someone would be selected in five days and the two remaining days were reserved for a short grieving period. It was the way it had always been, and she looked forward once again to a week at home. She told each of the soldiers she was proud of their service and told them to enjoy their week. This was the last action they would see for several months—at least she thought it was. Almost half the leaves had already fallen from the tree and soon it would stand barren. It would be hard to spy on the Grimmox with nowhere for them to hide. She was looking forward to the respite.

After dismissing her unit, she made her way to the commander's quarters because she owed them a report. She found a line of soldiers outside the commander's door and she joined it. The afternoon wore on as she waited and one by one; they went into the room and gave their final report. With every moment that passed, the anticipation grew and butterflies formed in the pit of her stomach. What would they react to her command's sighting? Would they have had her change her orders to stay any action? All these questions zoomed about in her mind, increasing her level of anxiety. Eventually, it was her turn, and a soldier led her into the quarters.

The commander looked up at her as she walked in. "Thula! How is my favorite soldier?" he asked.

The Final Offering

She couldn't help but smile. The more she spent in the commander's presence, the more she liked the man. Any question she had about his sincerity soon melted away and she opened up around him. That is until Silonia walked in and joined them.

The elder smirked as she walked with her hands behind her back, head held high, and took a position behind the commander.

Thula grew uncomfortable, but she needed to deliver her report. "I'm doing just fine, sir, thank you."

"Good, I'm glad to... I'm sorry, Silonia." He shifted his attention to the elder. "I didn't know you were coming in for the reports. In fact, you weren't as this is the first one you've attended and she is the second to last. Do you need something?"

Thula could see how the elder seethed. It appeared she wasn't used to someone questioning her. "I figured I would join in the report from our most promising young soldier. Tell me, Thula, how did your mission go?"

Figuring Silonia expected her to say they didn't spot anything, it delighted her to report otherwise. "Well, lady, we didn't see anything until three days ago. That's not to take anything away from my soldiers, though. They forayed farther into Grimmox territory than we were instructed to, and they did it without ever being spotted."

"I don't understand then." The commander furrowed his brow. "The other units had much more success and by barely getting into their territory."

"We were sent to watch an uninhabited area. We never spotted a soul and began to lose faith, but three days ago, that changed. I had one pair of troops three branches down, another pair had their back, and another pair took the rear. The remaining pair stayed back with me and monitored from above. We heard a rustle and my team hid."

Knowing she owed a full report, she continued to retell of the hunt they witnessed but left out the details about their unique rituals, as well as her instincts that the Grimmox seemed to know someone watched them. She wasn't sure what to make of them herself. The look of dismay on Silonia's face delighted her, and she couldn't have been more pleased.

"The following two days were quiet, and we didn't see the hunters again," she finished.

The commander was about to speak, but the elder cut him off. "So you're admitting you broke your orders? Your boldness knows no bounds, does it?" Silonia asked.

Thula curled her lip in anger. "While my troops followed my orders and went farther into enemy territory, we followed all protocol and weren't sighted. I don't see what the problem is."

"The problem is you didn't follow orders," Silonia said. "How can we continue placing trust in you, and your position, if you're not willing to follow the orders we're giving you?"

"I'm sorry. I'll make sure I don't stray from what you think is best going forward." She offered a fake smile. "My soldiers were restless and agitated since we hadn't seen anything yet. Given the relative quiet, I assumed it would be best if we proceeded farther to try to gather information. Maybe if we were

The Final Offering

given a better territory to observe, we wouldn't have had any issues."

"You will take whatever post we assign to you," Silonia said. "How dare you take that..."

The commander faced the elder and stopped her mid-sentence. "You're in no place to give orders here, Silonia. These are my troops and I have control over the ultimate decisions made." He turned and faced Thula. "I can understand the issues she faced, and while she went against the orders we issued, it is commendable she took the initiative. I've been in her position before, and if your soldiers think they are doing useless work, it can become easy for them to lose track of their mission and start making mistakes." He smiled. "I would've done the same thing. Well done, Thula."

"Thank you, sir." She bowed her head. At least someone saw her point and backed her up, but she wondered how Silonia would take this new development.

The commander glared at Silonia. "Is there anything else you need to report?"

She shook her head. "As I said, it was a pretty quiet post."

"We'll make sure we give you a better opportunity in the future. It doesn't do us any good to have one of our best sergeants away from everything going on. I had a different post assigned to you anyway, so it's disturbing my orders seem adjusted. Enjoy your time off and I look forward to putting you to work when you return."

She bowed her head again before turning and leaving his office. Feeling a sense of relief flood over her, she couldn't help but chuckle as the commander and the elder broke into a heated conversation as she closed the door.

The afternoon had arrived and a soft breeze blew what little heat remained in the fall air across her face. She walked out onto a limb and watched as several leaves lost their hold on the branch and fell toward the brown ground below.

Walking into the barracks, she packed up all her belongings. While she didn't expect her choice for the offering, one never knew and they were instructed to pack up since they were young, to be prepared just in case.

She fit all of her belongings into two bags and slung them onto her back before she took off for home. It would take her almost an hour to make her way down the tree, but her spirits were up just at the idea of sleeping in her own bed. After the events of the past several months, she longed for a week home with her family and friends.

Most of the other soldiers had already left as soon as they were dismissed, but several other sergeants and officers were just beginning the trek themselves. She saw Amridon with an officer. He was in a deep conversation but nodded to get her attention. He wanted her to wait, but she had no interest and started her descent down the tree. It was funny, she hadn't thought of Amridon at all while at her post, and wondered if he had thought of her. Maybe the distance between them was more permanent than just an assigned command. The train of thought bothered her, and she didn't know what to do next. She sighed and decided she would leave it in Halothias' hands.

It wasn't long before she heard the familiar noises of her village and her spirits lifted. She walked down the final stairs

The Final Offering

and noticed a buzz of activity. Guards stood throughout, and she was surprised to see several guarding the jade green chrysalis hanging from a branch in the middle of the village common square. A sudden flutter ran through her stomach, but she brushed it aside and made her way to her parents' home.

Walking in, she found her father, mother, and sister, Tilfin, all sitting on the couch. Dropping her bags, her mother ran up to her, and she embraced her as tears trickled down her face.

Her mother noticed. "What's wrong?"

She wiped away the tears and smiled. "I'm just glad to be home with people who love me."

Her father came up and hugged her too. "We're glad to have you home.

The Final Offering

Chapter 2

It was good to be home, and she could act like herself for the first time in a long time. Sleeping in her own bed like a baby, she woke up fresh and relaxed. She had planned a meeting with Alais and Myriani later in the day for lunch, so after breakfast, having nothing else planned, she decided she should get some exercise.

"I want to go for a run," she told her mother.

"Really, Thula?" her mother asked. "I can't remember a time when you would exercise for no reason."

Thula offered a smile to her mother. "What can I say? I have a routine now, and the last thing I want to happen is to lose all the endurance I've built up."

"I'm impressed," she said, "but you need to remember, you're on break. You seem to have aged several years in the short few months since joining the program. You need to relax a little too." Her mother gave her a comforting pat on her shoulder.

"There's nothing to worry about. I plan on taking advantage of my time off and will have plenty of relaxation," she said while chuckling.

She changed into her training clothes and walked outside. The morning air was cool, and gray clouds clogged the sky. Given the weather, she didn't expect to see the sun, a perfect day for a run.

With no destination in mind, she set out at a casual pace with no reason to rush. She took a meandering course, but soon grew bored and picked up her pace. With the leaves gone from the tree, she had a view of the entire horizon in all directions. Her breathing remained steady, but beads of sweat formed on her forehead. An encroaching branch from the neighboring aspen tree filled her vision, and she headed in its direction. After increasing her speed, she leaped onto the other branch. Everything faded away as she bounded from branch to branch. There was something about running that took her mind off the worries of everyday life. She felt comfortable and re-energized and continued running as the morning slipped by.

Ignoring the cluster of Haloti in the town square, she ran home, showered, and changed before heading out to meet her friends. They were waiting for her, sitting on a blanket with a basket. At her approach, they jumped up and ran to her.

"Thula!" Alais said. "I'm so glad to see you."

The Final Offering

Myriani hugged her. "You're home!"

"I can't tell you how great it is to be back." She embraced them both.

"Come, come join us for lunch," Alais said as they pulled her toward the blanket.

"Tell me, what's been going on?" she asked.

"You can't do that." Myriani chuckled. "We want to hear everything that's been going on with you."

"I'm sure you have many stories for us," Alais said.

Thula rolled her eyes. "I'll get to that, but I don't want to think about the program right now. I'm trying to forget about it, if only for a moment. Are you still dating one another?"

Alais took Myriani's hand in her own. "Of course we are. Don't you think we would have led with that if we weren't?" They both giggled.

Her friends described everything she missed in great detail. Not much had happened except the added guards and military buildup. They also described the arrival of the caterpillar. This year's creature had a reddish-brown body with bright yellow-green diamonds on its back. It arrived ten days ago and spun the jade-green chrysalis now hanging in the town square. It seemed this year's butterfly would be a blue morpho. This meant the Haloti would be in for a record harvest—good news for the village.

After her friends caught her up on the details of the village, they pressed her further for news about the Grimmox.

"Unfortunately, we only saw a Grimmox once. Otherwise, it was a boring three weeks," she said.

"You actually saw one?" Myriani asked.

"What did it look like?" Alais pleaded for more information. "Are they as ugly and monstrous as we've heard?"

"I saw two of them, and to be honest they look just like us—with a lighter shade to their skin that is."

They both looked perplexed. "The same as us, how can that be?" Alais asked.

"It's hard to explain, but if I didn't know any better, I would say we're related. You'd have to see them with your own eyes to understand what I'm saying."

"If they're as bloodthirsty as I've heard, I don't want to see one," Alais said, cringing into Myriani's side.

"That's just it. I don't think they are. We watched them hunt, and they were anything but aggressive or 'bloodthirsty'. We even caught them praying for the spirit of the dead animal. It was really…" she paused searching for the right word…"moving." She continued explaining everything she had witnessed to the delight of her two friends.

"I don't understand," Alais said. "If they're as peaceful as you say, then why are the elders causing such a commotion? Do you believe they're lying to us?"

"I went into the program hoping this wasn't the case. But the more I saw and heard during our training, the more I question their motives." She frowned. "I'll need more information before I jump to any conclusions." She didn't want

The Final Offering

to go into all that had transpired with Silonia; she wasn't sure how much they should know and wanted to protect them.

They prodded her more as they ate their lunch, but there was nothing more to offer.

After they finished eating, Myriani asked, "What about you and Amridon? I haven't seen the two of you together since you both returned."

"I wish I had better news to report on that front." Tears welled up in her eyes.

"What do you mean? Did something happen?" Alais asked. Both of her friends moved in closer to comfort her.

"No, it's fine. It's just that I thought our joining was destined. I've loved him since we were children." She looked at them both with red-rimmed eyes. "Well, you both already know that," she sniffed. "Once we arrived for training, he changed. He was no longer the loving and caring man we grew up around. He turned into a creature determined to exact revenge without a thought toward truth or integrity.

"One evening—it was the evening when I was attacked—he arranged for a private dinner between the two of us. He tried to explain himself to try to smooth things over between us, but suddenly he snapped."

The tears flowed from her eyes again. "His face changed, and when I looked into his eyes, I noticed they were no longer his—as if his very essence had disappeared. When I stared at them, I saw an empty soul, and the words dripping from his tongue stung me. They stabbed my aching heart and opened the already bleeding wound even further. I stormed off, but I noticed his eyes had returned to their normal state. Looking at him again—the real him—but it was too late. I couldn't be around him and headed back to the barracks. That's when I was attacked."

The girls were shocked; it showed all over their faces. "Amridon would never do anything to hurt you," Alais said.

"I just can't imagine, and then you were attacked. I mean, it must have killed him to see what happened to you," Myriani added.

"I was fine, but he showed his concern," she paused as sadness overwhelmed her. "Still, it can never go back to the way it was. Too much damage has been done."

"I'm sorry to hear that." They both put a supportive arm over her shoulders.

They continued prodding for more information, and she placated them as best as she could. When her friends seemed satisfied, they moved on to lighter topics and spent the rest of the afternoon reminiscing. They tried to cheer Thula up, as much as they could and guided the conversation onto anything other than Amridon and the Grimmox. It worked for a little while, but there was still a little voice in the back of her head, that kept bringing the painful subjects back to the forefront of her thoughts. She enjoyed the time though. It was just what she needed and what she had hoped for when she came home for the break.

The Final Offering

Chapter 3

A storm rolled in, evident by the dark green and gray clouds filling the sky. She could see lightning far off in the distance, and an occasional faint rumble near the foothills to the west. The winds had picked up and shook the branch. What few leaves remained on the tree the breeze carried off, dancing and floating on the swift currents.

She left Alais and Myriani after a restful afternoon. Wanting to beat the storm, she rushed toward her home. As she neared the village square, she spotted several guards surrounding the chrysalis of the butterfly. Several elders also stood near. Two of them had their hands placed on the jade-green material, and it looked as if they were muttering an incantation. This was something she had never seen before. She crept nearer to see if she could uncover anything, but out of the corner of her eye, she spotted Silonia. The elder grinned and made her way over to Thula.

"Are you enjoying your time off, Thula?" She bared her yellow and crooked teeth. Thula felt the full effects of a foul stench coming from her aged mouth. "I hope the events of the past month haven't been too much for you to overcome," she said with mock concern.

Thula put on her best face. Silonia seemed to show up everywhere she went, and she hated it. "I am enjoying it, elder. It has been very relaxing and is a real chance to recharge. It's just what I needed."

Thula watched as Silonia's greasy smile almost dropped from her face. "Good. We'll need you at full strength when you return." The elder turned and looked at the gathering around the chrysalis, then moved in closer to Thula, dropping her voice. "I hope you remember everything we discussed. It seems you have, don't think I haven't noticed your sudden change in demeanor, but I hope it isn't all for show."

"I meant everything I said to you at our little *meeting*. I hate the Grimmox and can't wait to take action against them. In fact, my soldiers had to hold me back when we spotted the two Grimmox hunting. I wanted to surround them and exact our revenge—teach them who they were messing with—but they talked me out of it by telling me it would go against our orders." It was difficult to lie, but she put all the anger she had toward Silonia into her fake hatred for the Grimmox.

"Good, it seems you have come around," Silonia said. Thula couldn't help but think Silonia suspected she lied. It was

The Final Offering

written all over her face, and the grin she tried to stifle didn't help matters either.

Thula tried to step away from her, but the elder only pulled her in closer. Thula cringed. "What are they doing around the offering chrysalis?" Thula asked.

The elder chuckled. "This is a ritual we hold before the offering. We communicate with the butterfly trapped inside to show it the process." She turned her head and stared into Thula's eyes. "It isn't a coincidence they always come out on a specific date at a specific time. We tell it when." Her eyes filled with complete malice.

This struck a chord with Thula as something occurred to her. "If you can communicate with it, what else do you instruct it to do?" she asked.

Silonia let out a hearty laugh. "You have to remember that this is a butterfly we are talking about. We don't communicate with it such as we are both doing right now. Their brains aren't advanced enough. We talk to it every day, trick its mind into thinking the time hasn't yet come. It is a method that kind of massages the chrysalis, setting it back in its process." She paused. "But no, we don't *communicate* with it exactly."

Thula didn't know if she believed her. After all, everything the elder spoke seemed to be a lie, but she grew revolted by her presence and needed to get away from her as fast as possible.

"That makes sense," she said. "Thank you for explaining it to me. I need to be heading home though. A storm is blowing in and I promised my mother I would help her prepare dinner. My sisters are both coming over."

The elder bowed her head to her as Thula turned and walked away, feeling Silonia's glare through her back. She was very aware something wasn't adding up, she just didn't know what. She sped up as raindrops fell from the sky and made her way to her parents' home, which of course was deserted. Her parents wouldn't be home for the evening. She made her way to her room and collapsed into her chair, reflecting on everything she had learned over the course of the afternoon. There was something needling at her from the back of her mind, but she couldn't put her finger on it.

The Final Offering

Chapter 4

After the run and meeting with her friends, she decided not to exercise the rest of the week, and instead took the time to find herself. She hated that she had signed up for the program, especially considering she had joined to be with Amridon, and things seemed irreconcilable. Not that he hadn't tried, though; he had come by every day trying to make up for everything he had done—although he still didn't understand what it was. That much was clear every time she sent him away.

The week had flown by and she didn't like that in a few days she would be back at her post. Undoubtedly, she would work closely with Amridon, and of course, Silonia. Thula had done her best not to focus much on these things, but every time her mind had a free moment, there they were again. Time continued to march on whether she was a willing participant or not.

The day of the offering had arrived. Tonight someone would be selected and whisked away, never to be seen or heard from again. Sometimes she wished for the selection, even if it meant her certain death. Things would be easier and she wouldn't have to be living her life full of lies, but that was just too easy. Halothias would never make it that uncomplicated on her. She had excelled in her training program, and the commander had placed her in a position of respect. No, things would never be that simple, and even if they were, would she want it that way? Every day was a reminder she had wanted this, had put herself in this position to figure things out. With nothing else to do, she put on a brave face and moved forward.

Her mother was on the committee overseeing all the food for the evening's dinner and offering. While the event was a somber one, it had become a tradition to hold a large feast to honor the memory of the yet-to-be-selected offering and send them off with a stomach full of home-cooked food. Her mother asked Thula to aid her and the others with the cooking duties. Thula obliged to help take her mind off everything else.

Shortly before lunch, she arrived, and they put her to work cleaning, peeling, and cutting vegetables. They were feeding the entire village, so this meant hundreds of vegetables. She cut the tips of her fingers several times on the sharp knife they provided, but she didn't mind. For the first time all week, her mind drifted away from her situation.

She enjoyed the camaraderie the women of the village shared. They told stories, and remembered lives; she learned of

The Final Offering

the history of her people. Almost every woman in attendance had lost someone over the years, and the air grew thick with the painful memories. Tears flowed throughout the afternoon. Never before had she been around so many strong women, and she realized they were the glue holding the village together. She gained a lot of respect for her mother and her friends that day.

After they cut all vegetables needed, she moved to bread duty. The dough was already mixed and set aside for rising. Her job was to prepare the dough for baking. Several large, makeshift, clay ovens had been set up, and already the heat coming from them was unbearable. She didn't mind though; she was just thankful to be doing something useful.

Before placing the dough into several plans for the final baking, she punched and kneaded it. Each time she plunged her hands into the gooey, warm dough, she imagined it was the face of Silonia and she took out all her aggression. In fact, several of the ladies joked with her, asking what the poor dough had ever done to her. She didn't care if she was the butt of the joke. All her anger built up, and she was relieved to take it out on something.

With the bread done—which she was sad about because she had more anger to dish out—they released her to enjoy what little remained of the afternoon. She had spent enough time with her friends over the past several days and didn't wish to run into Amridon, so she retreated home. Looking at the sun, she had just enough time to shower and clean up before the ceremony would begin.

The night before, she selected a deep green, silk gown, thinking it fit given the color of the chrysalis, and laid it out on her bed. Filling her basin with water, her muscles relaxed and unwound as she wiped away all the dirt and grime of the day. The cold water seemed to pull the stress out of her body and brought clarity to her mind. It felt good, and she relished every moment of it. When she finished, she noticed a gray ring around the top of the otherwise white bowl.

She emptied and cleaned it before sighing; she knew it would be a long and emotional evening. Since she had been through this many times before, she wasn't naïve and more than likely one of her friends would be the offering on this unusually warm evening. She put on her silk gown as her parents arrived home. They had very little time and would rush to get themselves prepared. Her mother had been cooking all day while her father was busy setting up tables and building the dais where the governor and his cabinet would sit for the evening.

She approached her mother and offered to help her clean up and get dressed.

"Thank you, Thula. I let the afternoon slip away from me." Her mother spotted her daughter's appearance for the first time since arriving home. "You look lovely." A tear formed at the corner of her eye. "I've never been more proud to be your mother."

"I had a good teacher." She smiled. "What can I help you with?"

Her mother cleaned up and Thula selected a red dress for her to wear. They walked down to the village square and looked for a place to sit. Her parents moved toward Amridon's family, assuming it would be what she wanted, but she tugged on her father's sleeve, redirecting him with her eyes to a table on the other side of the gathering.

The Final Offering

The scents of roasting meat and vegetables wafted on the breeze bringing saliva to her mouth. They sat next to a couple old friends beneath the bright, full moon that washed the entire village in an orange glow. Course after course arrived until they were all satiated.

It wasn't long before they brought out dessert, consisting of several types of berry pie. As they ate their pie, Governor Linotas stood and rang a bell to get the audience's attention.

"I would like to welcome everyone to our annual tradition that has come to be known as the offering. It is a sad, but necessary evil that has kept the Grimmox at bay for generations."

Quiet settled over the audience as they listened intently. "I've served the Haloti in my role for forty years, and it has been my honor, but I cannot take it anymore. It is with great sadness I announce I am resigning from my post." Murmurs erupted throughout the audience.

He waved his hands to quiet them down. "Assistant Governor Mycell will succeed me following the winter thaw. I have the utmost confidence in her as my successor; she has served in her current role for the past decade." A round of applause ran through the crowd as Mycell stood.

"I owe you all an explanation as to why." This comment drew the evil eyes of the elders, but he pressed on. He appeared troubled by the glares emanating from the elders and Thula assumed he would have to deal with their ire later in the evening. "The simplest explanation I can offer lays at the answer to this riddle."

If you break me, I'll not stop working,

If you can touch me, my work is done,

If you lose me, you must find me with a ring soon after.

What am I?

Silence fell on the crowd as they considered his words. They were thought-provoking and everyone shifted to look at one another, ruminating on the thoughts for several moments, while the governor waited for an answer. A young man finally blurt out, "Heart. The answer is heart."

The governor smiled. "Very good, yes the answer is heart. I've sat up here and watched forty children whisked away as a sacrifice to keep our enemies at bay. I've watched the families of the children grieve as they've dealt with their loss, I've even tried to comfort many of them, consoling them and telling them everything will be all right. But I've always known it wasn't right." He lowered his head, seeming to choose his next words with care.

"There's no reason we should go through this antiquated routine every single year, but the council disagrees with me. The elders have explained that this is the only way. They feel it is a small consequence and is something we're bound to from the ancient times. Given the recent events, the elders believe it's more crucial now than ever to keep them at a distance. Since I disagree, I'm doing the one thing my conscience will allow, and that is to resign my post.

"My heart hasn't been in this job for a long time, and it weighs heavy with all the innocent children I've sent away… forever. So this is the last offering I will oversee; the last child I will send off to their ultimate demise; the last family I will have

The Final Offering

to comfort as they deal with the loss of a loved one. I'm not in a position to make a change..."

Several elders motioned to the guards who rapidly approached the governor to stop his rambling before it caused any more damage.

"But it's not too late for you. The power has always been with the people," he yelled as the guards dragged him away. "It is time for you to stand up against this council and demand a change… it's time for…" They stuffed a piece of cloth into his mouth so he couldn't speak any longer.

The guards took him away, disappearing into his residence as the door slammed shut.

Speaker Tremalo stepped forward. "Yes, well, that was rather disturbing." He chuckled, though his voice betrayed his emotions. "The elders and I have known for a quite a while the governor struggled with his position, which is why we asked him to step down. His little show this evening was his way of getting back at us. Please disregard what he said, it has no relevance to the current situation."

His words hit each member of the audience, but whether they were convincing enough was yet to be seen. "Please, I invite you to finish your desserts before the true event begins."

Some ate their food as though nothing had happened. Others moved the food around their plates; their appetites suddenly vanquished. The already somber mood grew thicker and more foreboding as the weight of the evening fell on each of their shoulders. If nothing else, it felt like somehow and in some way, things would change in the future. It was only a matter of time now.

The Final Offering

Chapter 5

Several clouds rolled in front of the moon, obscuring its bright glow if only for a few moments. The wind died down, and the air grew quiet. The speaker walked up to the dais and two elders pounded on twin drums on either side of him. Everyone's attention shifted to the speaker.

"My dear Haloti, the time has come." His eyes shifted to the chrysalis sitting behind him as it moved from side to side. The drums continued their beat although at a softer cadence. "Let us watch the magical magnificence as this creature completes its transformation."

The crowd observed in fascination, this was the only part of the event that captivated people's attention. It was a blessing to watch one of the planet's most magnificent metamorphoses. Each transformation was different depending on the breed of the butterfly. It had been several years since they had had the chance to witness a Blue Morpho go through its transformation.

The chrysalis rocked back and forth, slowly at first but picking up speed as time went on. The top pulsed rhythmically, sending vibrations down its length. A crack appeared in the middle and they could faintly see the head of the butterfly waiting to emerge from its home. The pulsing picked up in intensity and the crack in the shell spread. With each vibration, the crack deepened further and further. One antenna popped free, followed by the other, and eventually, the head broke through. They could see the first glimpse of wings.

The butterfly continued to struggle and force its way free from the silk casing of the chrysalis. They pooped out at last. The tops rimmed in a dark black and filled with a deep blue growing lighter in color as it moved closer to its midsection. The underside was a mixture of brown and orange. The wings were small and still smoothed back; it couldn't move them yet. Not only did it not have the strength, but also they would collapse under the weight of the creature.

The abdomen was the last part to exit the chrysalis—large and bloated from the fluid filling it—the very fluid that would allow the butterfly to take flight. The Blue Morpho climbed out onto what remained of the chrysalis and rocked back and forth. As it moved, the abdomen shrank and its large blue wings were set to expand. Slowly the creature's abdomen returned to its realistic size, and shortly thereafter, it flapped its wings. With a little practice, it looked ready to try flight.

The Final Offering

It climbed into the sky and circled the Haloti in the village. They collectively held their breath as they knew soon one of their own would be carried off. Thula looked up in hypnotized amazement as the creature circled, flapping its powerful wings. When it seemed confident in its abilities, it dove closer to the branch where it flew one more circle. After finding its target, it flew even lower, almost skimming the heads of the Haloti. It neared Thula and buffeted its wings to slow its approach. It stopped directly above her head and reached down with its legs to pick her up.

Her eyes widened. *This is it,* she thought. *I'm being pulled away from everything I know.* Fear and apprehension stormed through her body as she forced herself to accept what was happening to her. And truth be told, joy coursed through her body too, knowing she would be released from the hell she'd been living for the past several months. She looked at her parents while the butterfly carried her into the sky. Fear and pain filled their faces as they watched their daughter. It flew her to the dais where it deposited her next to Tremalo. She hadn't noticed before, but Silonia and her commander had joined him. The grin on Silonia's face told the whole story.

Speaker Tremalo stepped forward as she regained her footing and the butterfly flew higher into the air. "The offering has been chosen." The drums stopped, and the air grew eerily quiet. "Thula, daughter of Cellomes and Gorven, you have been chosen by nature to help us stave off the threat known as the Grimmox. Your life here may end, but your spirit will live on for eternity. Halothias will welcome you with open arms as you are ushered into whatever may await you in your next life. As you are carried away and you take one last look at your home, know your sacrifice won't be in vain. Take comfort in the fact your family will forever be taken care of."

Somehow, Thula doubted that. Her nerves sizzled with anticipation, anxiety, and disbelief, somehow all comingling as the speaker whistled and the butterfly flew down. She shifted her gaze through the crowd, trying to make sense of the events taking place. Somehow she wasn't shocked, it made sense when she gave her mind a chance to catch up with her pounding heart. Of course, they wanted her out of the way, and what better opportunity than the offering. No one would question it. It was just too perfect. But how did they get the butterfly to choose her? Was that the *communicating* Silonia had been alluding to?

As the Blue Morpho neared, the commander reached out and grabbed Thula's arm, pulling her in closer.

"So very disappointing. You were one of the most promising recruits we have ever seen, but you threw it all away." She didn't understand the commander's words at first. He continued to stare stoically into the crowd as he whispered poison into her ear.

"Even after I told Silonia to bring you in to talk sense to you, you still continued your private endeavors—though you were more secretive about it. At least you gave us the perfect excuse to build up our military. I guess we can thank you for that."

Her eyes grew large and her skin tingled as understanding filled her mind. The commander was working with Silonia and she never even noticed. She felt childish and overmatched, not understanding how she had allowed this to happen.

The Final Offering

The commander lowered his voice further, hissing. "She warned you we had ways of dealing with miscreants such as yourself, but you didn't listen. Your stubbornness was too much to overcome, and you forced us to take you out of the equation. I hope you enjoy whatever awaits you in the clearing." With disgust filling his face he moved away from her.

The butterfly picked her up and rose higher, stalling in the air over the entire square so she could get one last look. Her parents embraced one another, and her mother's face shimmered with wetness from the tears streaming down. Her father had been crying too, his face puffy and reddened. Suddenly the butterfly turned and flew past the aspen tree and circled around the cedar tree for several moments. Coming alive for the first time in awhile, she found her voice and shrieked as they flew away. Her home disappeared before her eyes and she felt empty and hollow. The wish to live left her and even her screams faded away unheard in her throat.

They circled the cedar tree several times and the muscles in her shoulders ached where the butterfly's legs dug into her. She hadn't known what to expect, but this wasn't it. If she was to die, she hoped it would happen soon.

Confusion filled her as she looked around and tried to find where they headed. *Where are the Grimmox? Aren't they supposed to be involved since this is the whole reason they hold off attacking us?* At least that was what they had always been told.

She suddenly grew terrified as the butterfly took flight to the south, leaving all the trees well behind them. Everything she had known her whole life disappeared, and she had no idea what was in store for her. *What if the Grimmox offering is a complete lie, and this is just a way of getting rid of me?* Her thoughts circled with a fury at what awaited her.

Then, as suddenly as her terror had arisen, a calmness flooded her mind. Thoughts? No, that wasn't really the right term as she didn't hear or see anything, but soothing emotions flooded her body and the tension vanished.

After a short distance, they descended. She heard the rhythmic trickle of a river grow louder as they neared the ground before she finally saw the wide body of water stretched out before them, reflecting the silver rays of the moon. The scene was tranquil, and she allowed it to calm her body as the butterfly dropped her on the ground.

Is this really what happens? She thought. *Are they going to drop me off out here in the middle of nowhere to fend for myself?*

In her mind, she was frightened, but the soothing emotions still flooded her body as though she were drugged. When she should care, she didn't in the least.

Drink some fresh water. A voice said in her head. *It isn't yet time so we must wait. All must be asleep.*

Searching frantically, she turned around looking for the owner of the voice, but she couldn't see anyone.

There is no need to be frightened, Thula. I am your carrier.

Thula spun around and looked at the butterfly. It had landed on the ground next to her. She wasn't sure, but she thought she noticed a small bow of the head from the creature. Every one of her instincts was to scream out in fear, but the overwhelming

The Final Offering

calmness kept her emotions steady. It was all confusing. She wanted to speak but didn't know how.

Before she could try, the creature continued speaking directly into her mind. *You have no reason to worry. I'm taking you to a better place, but we must wait. I urge you to drink water. The emotions I'm sending to you have a way of dehydrating one's body.*

As if to emphasize the point, the butterfly crept closer to the river and drank greedily from the fast-moving current.

Following the creature's lead, she knelt and drank herself. She couldn't understand how she hadn't noticed the thirst creep up, but her mouth was dry and her throat ached as if on fire from within. Although her mouth was full, she couldn't seem to get enough, but her stomach filled and she stood. Unsure of how to communicate telepathically, she got up the nerve and tried to speak to it.

"Thank you for sending me the soothing thoughts. I fear I may have been a handful with the fear gripping my body."

It is the way of the offering. You are not the first, nor will you be the last. We have had many experiences and have learned a few things over the years.

She was sure this was the truth. For once, someone—or something for that matter—was finally being honest with her. "You haven't lived that long, how do you know what has transpired in the past?" she asked.

Once we deliver the offering, we return to the elders and relay what has been done. They, in turn, pass it on to each new carrier in later years.

"So you work for the elders? I would think something as magnificent as you would never work for despicable creatures such as them," she said with her bitterness palpable between them.

We have no choice, my Lady. It's an agreement reached between our two kinds generations ago. In exchange for our services, we are free to eat and transform in your lands without any fear of being hunted. There was a short pause. *However, I will agree your elders are loathsome creatures who should never be trusted.*

At least they had a strong understanding on that front. "How do you make your choice? What do you look for?" she asked.

I must warn you, we are reaching the limit of what I'm allowed to share. However, I will tell you we are instructed as to whom to select by the elders, and we have your scent. They send us images along with the information from the past over the course of several days. This is not a random act; we are following orders. They even offer us a sample of your blood. That way we can pick you out in a crowd. It may smell like the earth to you, but to us, it is a unique scent.

"I knew it!" she blurted out. "But what happens to me now?" Thula tried to hold on to the calm feelings from before, but it was increasingly difficult with all the new knowledge flooding in.

I'm afraid I have nothing further to offer you. As I said before, I'm taking you to a better place and I will reveal it all over time. Your emotions will stay calm as long as you stay near me. My body emits an odor that naturally inhibits the emotions

The Final Offering

of fear and trepidation. Be free to take time to reflect and meditate. We have a little time yet to wait, but we will be back on our way before you know it.

Bowing her head to show her respect, she said, "I thank you for being so gentle with me, and for answering my questions."

Walking over to a rock resting on the edge of the river, she sat down. The evening air so close to the water brought a chill to her skin. She brought her legs closer to her chest to keep in her body heat. For the first time, she remembered she was wearing a dress and felt exposed, but there was nothing she could do about it now.

She stared long and hard at the moon and became transfixed by the dark spots looking down at her. It seemed as though she entered a trance-like state. All care drifted away from her mind and she saw clearly for the first time without any reticence.

In an almost amused state, she realized she had been right all along. The elders had lied to her; had lied to them all for generations, and they deserved a swift punishment to atone for their transgressions. She just didn't know how it would be possible now.

Suddenly something nudged her arm. She looked over and saw the butterfly standing right next to her.

The time has come, Thula. Prepare for flight.

"Already?" Her gaze shifted to the blackness of the sky. The moon had traveled far from where it had been, and by her best guess, several hours had passed. "How long have we been sitting here?"

It has been almost three hours. Now, if you're ready.

Thula stood and let the creature grab her shoulders. *Three hours?* She thought to herself. *How can that be possible?* It felt as though only minutes had passed. However, she did feel well rested, as though she had slept a full night.

The butterfly gained altitude and carried her back to the north, back toward her home. She looked up and noticed the smooth motion of the creature's wings. They flapped gracefully, cutting through the cool evening air. She saw the outline of the cedar tree and her heart warmed. They passed quickly and dove beneath a branch of the aspen. Continuing their descent, the butterfly went for one of the lower branches of the sugar maple; the tree she had called home for the entirety of her life—although she had never been this far down before.

They leveled off and made a wide circle as if scouting it out before the butterfly landed.

I must make sure everyone is asleep. It would do no good for them to see me deliver you.

She tried to pry for more information from the butterfly, but it remained quiet as it made another circle, just to be sure. At this height, she couldn't believe how thick the branches were. Some of them doubled the size of the branches she called home. As they made the third circle, she spotted a cluster of orange lights glowing warmly in the blackness of the cold night. The light-filled a hollowed out knot deep in the trunk, between two large branches. If she had to wager a guess, she would assume this had once been the foundation of another branch, but it had been lost some time ago—evident by the deep black color filling the walls.

The Final Offering

As she expected, the creature headed straight for this knot. It was filled with several leaves that would give a thick, comfortable surface for her to spend the night. The butterfly gently deposited her in the alcove. It hovered just outside for a moment.

Welcome to your new home, Thula. This is where I must leave you. I hope this life brings you more joy than you ever experienced in your previous one.

"Wait! What am I supposed to do here? Do I venture out into this new territory?" she asked.

You will sleep. When you awake, you will find the answers you seek.

"Sleep? But how am I supposed to do that? I'm refreshed and well rested after our time by the river. Even if I wanted to, I don't think I could carry out the task."

I don't think you will have any issues. It has been a pleasure to be your carrier and I wish you nothing but prosperity as you move forward. The creature flew closer and rubbed its head gently against her cheek. It then backed up and disappeared into the black abyss of the night.

"But wait!" she called out. She needed to know more, and she had no intention of sleeping. Continuing to call out, her eyes grew heavy. She tried to fight it off, but they became as burdensome as lead weights pulling her lids down ever tighter. Unable to fight off the urge, she curled up into a ball and pulled a thick green leaf over her body to keep her warm. She drifted off into a dreamless sleep.

The Final Offering

Chapter 6

Thula opened her eyes and then shut them again as the bright rays from the sun filled her vision. She blinked while they slowly acclimated to the new light, and her sight came into focus. A tall, blond-haired individual stood in front of her. Afraid, she jumped back, struggling to push herself deeper into the knot she had slept in as if she was afraid he would attack her.

"Take it easy. I won't harm you." He smiled and reached out his hand to help her sit up. "I thought the butterfly used too much of its sleeping potion on you. Mid-morning has already come and gone. I was afraid you would never wake up."

Hesitant, she still wouldn't take his outstretched hand.

He pushed his arm closer to her. "Really, I won't bite." His smile persisted. "Oh, I guess it would help if I introduced myself to you. My name is Hetorian of the Grimmox, and I was sent to welcome you to your new home." He looked around before returning to her. His long hair blew in the soft breeze. "If you will accept my help, that is."

She stared long and hard at his face as she still refused. Her mind worked furiously to make sense of the scene before her. Squinting and thinking she had seen him before, but that couldn't be possible, could it? Then it dawned on her. He was one of the hunters she had seen at her former post. He didn't seem to recognize her, but then again, he had only looked at her out of the corner of his eye. Upon recognizing him, she outstretched her hand and allowed him to help her out of the knot.

He led her to the edge of the branch where he motioned for her to sit down. "I've told you my name, what's yours?" he asked.

She didn't know how much she trusted him as she wasn't used to being in the company of one with such light skin. As she sat down, she felt light-headed, as if all of her energy had drained from her body. To steady herself, she put her hand to her head. "My name is Thula."

He noticed how pale her skin had become; well as pale as one could get when they had darker skin. "I'm sorry, Thula, I completely forgot." Rummaging through a bag he carried, he pulled out a leaf-wrapped package and handed it to her. "Here, I'm sure your body is drained. Eat this and your energy will return."

The Final Offering

She grabbed it from his hands and unwrapped the package. Inside it looked like a biscuit, but it was heavy and contained green flecks throughout. Turning it over in her hands, leery of what she was putting into her body, she said, "Thanks." She took the plunge and bit into the thick biscuit. A sweetness filled her mouth, but she tasted several herbs too, and ravenously went in for another bite.

Hetorian smiled. "It's good, isn't it?" She nodded in agreement. "It's a secret recipe from our ancestors."

Between bites, she said, "Why am I so hungry? I ate a large meal last night, but it seems as though I haven't eaten in several weeks."

"It's the spells the butterfly used on you. They spend a lot of your excess calories. They serve a purpose—to keep you calm while they carry you here—but it leaves you very weak. With the manipulation of your thoughts, you don't even realize it. I should have remembered and been better prepared. For that, I apologize."

Finishing the last bite—it was so satisfying—she searched for the crumbs and licked them up. She was satiated and turned to look at Hetorian. "So what happens now? Will I be thrown into prison or something?" she asked.

"Throw you in prison?" he balked. "No, there will be no prison. We'll blend you into our society where you will be free to do as you wish."

She stared at him with wide eyes. "Then I wish to go home."

"I'm afraid that won't be possible. It would go against the long-standing treaty we hold with your people."

Knowing the answer before she asked, she had to ask anyway. "So just like that, you expect me to forget everything I've learned about your people?" Anxiety and anger waged a war inside her. *Which would win out*, she wondered in the back of her mind.

"I'm afraid your elders taught you very inaccurate information. Over the next several weeks, it will be my job to try to show you the truth. I'm not expecting you to throw away all you hold dear, that would go against everything we stand for, but we ask you stay open-minded. In fact, if you wish you can hold on to all of your old ideals. If you wish to continue to pray to Halothias, we won't hold you back. There are even many Haloti who've come here—just as you have—who set up a church and still hold to their old ways. You'll find we are amenable."

She had forgotten about the others, this piqued her interest. "Will I get to meet any of the other Haloti?"

"Of course, but in time. We don't wish to overwhelm you. Which is why the butterfly delivered you late at night while we were all asleep. We've learned the transition process works best when we acclimate you slowly." His face seemed to cloud over with sorrow. It was such a contrast to his vibrant smile, it made her take note. He continued, "Several of your kind took their own lives because they couldn't get used to their new home. It brought much pain and sadness before we realized the culprit." She was taken by surprise to see such a palpable ache exhibited on his face. "Now we assign one volunteer who handles walking

The Final Offering

the Haloti through the transition slowly." His warm smile returned.

She wondered at the complete empathy in his voice, and the concern filling his face when he spoke of the sad transition of her people. This was NOT the Grimmox she was told of her whole life.

Staring at him for a long moment, taking in the bright colors of his tattoos, she asked, "So is this your job then? Do you transition each offering? Is that what your tattoos have decided?" These questions occurred to her, even though she had an idea it was not his job since she had seen him hunting just a few days before.

"No, this isn't my job. In fact, we don't have jobs. We all volunteer for whatever task needs to be done. Everyone pulls their own weight and contributes to the betterment of the society. Right now, I'm tasked with transitioning you. Last week I hunted," he winked. "The week before that, I assisted with the harvest."

"What about your tattoos? And your military, don't you have soldiers?"

"Our tattoos? They don't mean anything. You're taught otherwise, but you'll come to learn that our tattoos," he moved his arms, "all of our kind's tattoos are nothing more than a unique identifier. We all have them and no two are alike. They're not the all-seeing, all-knowing view of who we are or what we are destined to do. We respect personal choice, and everyone serving one another."

She thought long and hard about it. "But I don't understand. Our whole society is built around our tattoos. How do you build up your military?" She looked perplexed.

"We don't have a military. There has never been a need. Our only enemy is the Haloti, and we've had a long-lasting peace between our two people."

"But a Grimmox was spotted in our territory. We're building up our military right now in response; preparing for the worst should you decide to attack us. Everything you're telling me is that you won't fight, but that goes against everything we've been raised with." She shook her head, trying to make sense of this new version of the Haloti's sworn enemy.

He chuckled. "We would never attack the Haloti. It is our hope, to one day unite with our brothers and sisters."

"Do you mean we're the same? But we look so different."

"Are we? The only difference I see is our skin tone," he paused. "We started our lives together and we hope to one day merge back together as one in nature. But this is a conversation for another day. I've been instructed to stick to the basics today, just enough to satisfy your simplest questions."

He turned his head and looked up and down her body, examining her own faint tattoos. "Tell me more about yourself. What is your job with the Haloti?"

She watched him as he studied her markings, blushing a bit as his gaze traveled her complete shape. She was uncomfortable under his scrutiny.

The Final Offering

"Well, as you can see my tattoos haven't come in yet, so I wouldn't have a job for at least another year. But, in response to the Grimmox sighting, the council of elders determined it was necessary to create a new program where volunteers would be trained in the art of espionage."

He didn't let her finish. "So you're a spy? Should I be concerned your choice as the offering was another act of espionage?" Concern filled his face.

"Yes, I am a spy, but I'm afraid you have nothing to worry about. My position as the offering was a form of punishment." She stood and walked further down the branch, examining her new view. Turning back, she said, "You see, I started to question the elders' intentions. It seemed to me they had other motivations. So I joined the program and hoped I could find out what was going on from the inside." She sat down with him again. "They saw right through me. When I grew too close to the truth, they used me and arranged a fake attack they worked to further their interests. It wasn't long before I was their poster-child, their reason to build up the military even more." Tears filled her eyes. "The offering couldn't have come at a better time and they took the opportunity to dispose of me. I can see it all very clearly now."

"It all makes sense to me too," he said solemnly. "I'm so sorry you've been pulled from all you know and discarded like a piece of refuse." He leaned closer and wrapped his arm around her. "It will be difficult, but I swear you'll feel at home here soon enough." Her earlier unease with him evaporated, much to her amazement.

Standing, he grabbed her hand, pulling her to her feet. "Let me show you to your new home so you can get settled before we go any further." He led her up the tree at a casual pace. "I must warn you, you might receive looks like you are the new one here. Don't pay it any mind. None of it is intended to be negative. It's just that you're a new face, that's all."

They wound their way up a smooth staircase carved into the trunk of the tree as he led her to her quarters. They climbed several other branches, and he showed her a bright red door. Everything looked so much like her own home. Then again, they were on the same tree so why shouldn't it?

"It isn't much, but it will serve for the time being. This home belonged to an elderly lady, who lost her husband several years ago. She passed away last month. There's no need to worry, it has been thoroughly cleaned and blessed. You're welcome to stay here as long as you wish. You can make it your permanent home, or you are welcome to find another that is more suitable to your needs." He smiled. "You didn't bring any belongings, but take a look around, clean up, and get comfortable. You'll find several outfits in the bureau that should fit you unless of course, you wish to stay in your dress."

"Thank you for your hospitality, Hetorian." She bowed and offered her gratitude. "Once I have changed and made myself more presentable, what comes next?" she asked.

"I need to check in with the governors—who you'll be introduced to in due time—to give an update on how everything has gone this morning. After that, I'll take a seat right over there." He pointed to a bench sitting in a courtyard across from her home. "I'll be patiently awaiting your return."

She watched as he disappeared into the crowd before turning and walking into her new home. The home sat dark and

The Final Offering

she couldn't help but feel like a stranger. It wasn't big, just a bedroom, kitchen, dining room, washroom, and common room, but it would suit her needs perfectly. Taking it all in, she ran her fingers over the tops of the furniture as she walked through her new accommodations. The way the last occupant had set up her home was charming. It felt comfortable and lived in, almost as if it were her own home. In many ways, the craftsmanship was similar to the fashion her parents preferred. This thought brought the painful realization she would never see her home again, and she was overwhelmed by a sadness creeping over her.

She made her way to the bedroom and opened the bureau. As Hetorian had said, the drawers were filled with many outfits. She selected a simple silk tunic and leather breeches and quickly put them on. Before opening her door, she took a deep breath, closed her eyes and told herself she was starting a new life. Exhaling and opening her eyes, she walked out in search of Hetorian.

The Final Offering

Chapter 7

She weaved in and out of people, making her way to the bench Hetorian pointed to earlier. Most of the Grimmox waved, smiled, or politely asked her how she was doing, but they didn't linger, ask questions, or make her uncomfortable. Other than their appearance, they went about their daily lives such as her own people had done her entire life. It helped to soothe her and went a long way toward making her more comfortable.

People milled about as she stopped and looked around. Within moments, she couldn't believe her eyes. Mixed among the Grimmox were several Haloti. Among them, she spotted several of all different ages, but what amazed her the most were the children. Not only were there many dark-skinned children, but she saw even more who looked to be a mix of the two, both Haloti and Grimmox. Taking a step back, she ran her hands through her hair. This was something she never expected and needed a moment to take it in. Then she chastised herself for being closed-minded. Of course, the Haloti would be sealed with whoever they loved, be it another Haloti or even a Grimmox. It had never crossed her mind, and she was a bit surprised to note it brought a smile to her face.

A smile filled her face when she made her way to the bench and found Hetorian already there awaiting her presence. He stood at her approach. "That was much quicker than I expected. Are you sure you don't need any more time?" he asked. "This is a lot to take in."

"What would I need more time for? She laughed at the ridiculousness of it all. "I have no belongings, no assigned job, no family or friends to take up my time. All I needed was a clean pair of clothes, which were already waiting for me in my room." It amazed her she was already so comfortable in his presence.

"Well good. Are you hungry, or do you need something to drink?"

"No, I'm good. Whatever was in the biscuit has filled me up." She looked around the common area. "So what else do we have in store?"

"You're handling things so well..." She could see the warmth in his bright blue eyes and could hear the sincerity in his voice. "Our first task is a history lesson. Time to unlearn all the untruths you've learned your whole life, but not here. There are too many people around and you seem to garner a bit of

The Final Offering

attention. If we stay, I'm sure we will face countless interruptions." He turned with a gleam in his eyes. "Follow me. I hope you can keep up."

He took off running, and she followed him. He bounded down the limb and used his wings to jump higher onto other branches. She kept pace with him and would have overtaken him had she known where they were heading. They climbed higher and higher as she wondered if they were going back to Haloti territory, but once they left the Grimmox village well behind them, he slowed and walked out toward the end of a well-secluded branch.

Inviting her to join him, he sat down. She looked up and realized they were still well below her home. She took a seat to Hetorian's right and awaited his words. He pulled out a canteen and offered her a drink. After the short run, she drank greedily of the cool water. Seeing her satiation, he took a couple swigs of his own.

"I'm not here to tell you everything you've learned has been wrong, nor am I here to debate anything with you. I've heard what you've learned and I understand what you think you know. I ask you to listen to what I have to say. If necessary, the proof will come later. You have every right to be skeptical, and I'm sure if we reversed our situations, I would be too."

She nodded. "I understand and will do my best to just listen." Again, she studied him, wondering about the boy, well man, behind the task of *transitioning* her. As much as she was already skeptical, she pushed this to the back of her mind and remained focused on the task in front of her.

"Thank you. That's all I ask." He paused and cleared his throat. "God created all that surrounds us. He provided shelter for us to live in to keep us out of the elements, and He provided food for us to eat—both plants that sprout up from the ground and animals roaming the plains. Everything you see was touched by Him and is all a part of His divine plan. The animals themselves are also His children, and when we take the life from one for our own consumption, we honor their life and offer a prayer He will welcome their spirit into His realm with open arms, in recognition of their sacrifice so we may live on.

"After creating this world, He wanted children to roam the plains and climb the trees. He gave to us four such children. Two sons, Halothias and Grimosias and two daughters, Trifana and Meliana. Halothias and Meliana found each other to be suitable mates, which left Grimosias and Trifana to create the second pair." Skepticism built on her face, but she honored her agreement and bit her lip to hold back her words.

"In the early years, both pairs procreated and filled our world. Both women gave the brothers ample children and the population boomed. There were different ideas of how the society should be built, and both brothers had to compromise. They settled on a democracy with all members participating in the responsibilities of maintaining the village.

"The society flourished for almost a generation, but as the brothers grew older, it seemed they would never agree, and had different ideas for the future of their little settlement. It wasn't uncommon to see them arguing and fighting in front of the other villagers, and a divide grew among the people. Although they shared the same God, their Father, they had very different views on how they should be seen as His sons.

The Final Offering

"Halothias argued that as the sons of God, they too should be viewed as gods in their own right. Grimosias argued that there could only be one God. After all, they populated the world and every member of their society was a direct descendant, meaning all citizens were direct descendants of God. This was not the vision their father had laid out for them.

"When both men neared the end of their lives, having graced this very tree for well over one hundred years—having sired the entire population—they finally agreed to disagree. On mutual terms, they decided the people could choose whichever line of thinking they preferred, and once decided, they agreed to part ways creating two different villages—the Grimmox and the Haloti.

"Long after the brothers died, the two villages turned on one another and centuries of war ensued as the division between the two continued to grow. Much of the population died during this time of war, but it appeared as though the Haloti were close to exterminating the entire race of Grimmox people. God was upset with the way things transpired, and in His frustration, He rained down record storms further ravaging the populations and He only made matters worse.

"Displeased with the actions of His two sons, He brought their spirits before Him and told them both to correct the mistakes they together had created.

"With both villages in disarray, Halothias and Grimosias returned to the planet and brought the two villages together. They ordered a truce and created a plan where the Haloti would claim the upper half of the tree, and the Grimmox the lower. Each village was forced to move and faced the reality of starting over once again. The brothers ordered them to mind their own business and keep to their own territories, or they would face the wrath of their celestial father, God.

"The two brothers departed the physical world and left the two villages to carry out their orders. Disappointed with their own actions, the Haloti elders agreed to send one of their own to live with the Grimmox as a sign of peace. This act served two purposes: first, it helped the Grimmox to reestablish their population as their numbers were far lower after the war. Second, it would hopefully prevent future generations of Haloti from ever attacking the Grimmox again, as now their people would be mixed. The elders of both races came together once a year to review how the arrangement was working. If any adjustments were necessary, they would change things for the betterment of both races.

"For many years this arrangement worked as planned. In fact, the Haloti and Grimmox moved between the two villages. There was a peace and harmony between them that rivaled what it had been like when they all lived together. Of course, as with many things in life, it seemed too good to be true. Corruption and dissension grew over the next several generations.

"The two villages, who had now helped each other out for years, seemed to grow further apart. One day, they made a decision that any Grimmox within Haloti territory would be ushered out by armed guards. The council of Haloti elders approached the Grimmox and told them not to ever come into their territory again.

"The Grimmox expected the terms of their original agreement to have become null and void, meaning there would no longer be an exchange of a Haloti youth. However, on a fall morning, much as today was, a youth arrived. He was only

The Final Offering

thirteen and was fearful for his life. Relaying everything, he proudly exclaimed he was the first *offering*. Every year they heard the new stories, and it seemed the Haloti elders had continued with their age-old agreement, but they had transformed it into a tool; a tool they used to instill fear and keep their people in line, and away from the Grimmox.

"From what our own council could determine, they formed lies and painted the Grimmox as monsters who demanded a sacrifice in exchange for their compliance with the new terms of the agreement. Our elders approached the Haloti and tried to return the children, but they sent them away and were told never to return. The Haloti no longer wanted the children, and the elders said if the children ever returned, they would be killed in an act of defiance. This was the new agreement and there would be no variance from what they outlined." He took a deep breath and let the air out slowly, giving Thula a chance to absorb all he had told so far.

Hetorian plunged on. "Year after year they heard the new tales as a new Haloti child arrived, and each year they noticed how much more fearful the arriving youth was. We welcomed each child into our village trying everything we could to make the transition easy. We did this to make them feel welcome and at home as one of our own. We never wanted anyone here against their will or afraid for their life." He lifted his hands and dropped them in his lap. He looked desolate. Thula noticed again the hurt he displayed for these perfect strangers.

"It hasn't always been easy, and as I mentioned before, several of your own kind have gone so far as to take their own lives; reconciling the two tales being too difficult for them. But with each death, we learned, and we created a program that would make it easier for you as you digested the information and assimilated into our own culture." He finished speaking and looked at Thula. Her eyes were red and her face was damp with tears.

He looked as though he expected a response, or at the very least some questions, but she sat in silence, deep in thought. As he waited patiently, she stood up and walked away. She traveled down to the end of the branch and screamed. Looking down at the ground, she bounced on the balls of her feet as if she were about to leap. Hetorian apparently had seen enough and came after her, frantically yelling her name.

The Final Offering

Chapter 8

He ran to the edge of the branch. "Thula!" he shouted. "Please don't jump."

She turned and faced him as he ran up, confusion crossing her face. "Jump? I wasn't going to jump. It's just that... I... I..." she started sobbing again.

He pulled her in close and smoothed her hair as she let the tears flow, burying her face in his chest. "It's difficult to hear, but I promise everything I've shown is the truth. It just takes time to get used to."

She pulled back and wiped the tears away from her face. "No, that's not it at all. I believe you. I believe everything you said. All you did was confirm my own suspicions. It's just that suspecting something and finding out it's the truth is difficult to take all at once."

"What do you mean you suspected these things?" He looked at her with concern. "No Haloti has ever come here knowing the truth."

"As I said before, the whole reason I'm here is that I questioned the elders' intentions. We go through life with blinders over our eyes and accept the word of people like them because they are in a position of power. I watched as my friends—those I loved and held dearest—plainly accepted everything the elders said as the unabashed truth. I took the time to listen to what they were saying, and little by little it stopped making sense."

He nodded and opened his mouth to speak, but stopped. Sometimes the best way to help an emotional person was to let them speak; to get it all out so they could move on and begin the healing process.

"Take the Grimmox sighting for instance. Why would you venture into our territory, after all of these years, and not do anything? Only one person claimed to have seen him, and it was the middle of the day. Realistically, someone else would have at least caught a glimpse, but no. There was no one else. Then the sudden change in procedures. It seemed too convenient and too quick. They implemented it at once."

He was all ears and sat back as he listened to her mind whip and whir as if connected to a finely tuned machine.

She laughed a sarcastic guffaw before she continued, "I mean we all know how slowly the council moves, even when it's in their best interest. They would've needed time to create

The Final Offering

the plans, and get the military to sign off on them. It would have taken weeks, but at the end of the discussion, they placed tables with officers at the ready to take the names of the volunteers.

"When we started the espionage program after completing basic training, they stuck us in a classroom and thought, 'who better to lead a class than an elder', which also made no sense. Someone in that position would never accept such a lowly job. I'm sorry, anyone could argue with me, but the fact is all elders are arrogant—at least the Haloti elders." She shot him a look, the first one in her whole tirade so far. "They've been in their positions far too long and have gained too much power. They don't want to babysit newbie recruits. Why would one of the most prominent elders take on the role of the teacher? They wouldn't." She shrugged her shoulders and paced furiously. Her mind ran at break-neck speeds trying to process everything that now made so much sense.

"But it all became clear as soon as the first class started. They needed an elder because she would be the only one capable of brainwashing us. Because, let's face it, that's all it was. Nothing but propaganda dripped off the tongue of Silonia. I doubt I was the only one not falling for it, but I raised my barriers and was skeptical. Never did I think it would land me here, but they spotted me and aimed to make an example of me.

"They did everything they could to work me." She shook her head in grim acceptance. "They created a divide between Amridon and myself and used the connection we shared as a weakness. Amridon was weak-minded and easily swayed. They used him against me as he grew further and further intertwined with the program. I still don't know how, but they even programmed him to question my motives."

She rounded on Hetorian, "Sick, right? When that happened, it was over. My life would never be the same and the divide between Amridon and myself had grown too large to heal, so they used that. They used me at my weakest." Her fury spent, tears glistened in her eyes as she recalled the situation with a stab of pain, her voice softened as anger mingled with sadness.

"You see, I had a bitter fight with Amridon—we courted one another in case that wasn't clear by now—and as I walked home, they arranged for an attack. But, I didn't sustain any serious injuries, nothing but a bug bite…"

Suddenly, dawning fell across her face. She remembered what the butterfly had said. Something stood out now she had casually skipped over the night before.

Hetorian looked confused as she continued to work things out on her own.

"Sorry, I remembered something the butterfly told me last night. Something I didn't catch before, but now that I can see clearly, I've put all of the pieces together. I always understood the reasoning behind the attack I sustained, but I never could figure out the wound on my neck. I remembered them stabbing me with a device, but the physicians told me it was a bug bite, so I brushed it off and pushed it out of my mind.

"Last night the creature—the butterfly—told me the elders sent clear pictures to it while in the chrysalis, of what I looked like."

She stopped, spun around, narrowed her eyes at him, "That's not what is important here, but I'm trying to work through this in real-time, so bear with me while I process." He

The Final Offering

nodded his support, seemingly patient with her ever-turning tides.

"It also told me the elders sent it a sample of my blood. That way, it had my scent and could easily pick me out in a crowd. I assumed they gave it some of the blood they took from me when I first enrolled in the program. However, I enrolled over eight months ago and there is no way a sample would still be viable. Nor would they have saved it anyway. They wouldn't have known the course we would walk down, now would they? As part of the attack, they took my blood. They had to. They needed the butterfly to find me and no one else in the crowd at the offering.

"I wonder." She paused as she thought a little more. "I wonder if all the other Haloti offerings had a similar experience. I may have to ask them once I'm more comfortable here, and they with me."

He offered her a smile as she relaxed. Putting the pieces together, she came to terms with everything that had happened to her.

"Anyway, I'm getting off on a tangent and none of this is important, so I'll go back to where I was heading before I remembered the information from the butterfly." She picked up her pacing again. It certainly helped her process.

"It's not a problem, Thula. I'm glad you're working through it all, it will help."

"The attack, and the way the news spread thereafter provided the perfect opportunity for them to put even more of their plans into action. They blamed the attack on the Grimmox...well, your people, and used it as a reason to build up the military even more. They placed guards throughout the city and asked for more volunteers—they even suspended the placement based on our tattoos even further to accommodate any young Haloti who wished to join. They needed the young since there wouldn't be the numbers necessary to accommodate their attack strategy using the current military units.

"All the while, they used me as a poster child to advance their propaganda. I'm a young woman, true enough, but one trained. I went through basic training and passed with flying colors; I even earned special recognition. I had also completed the special espionage training and should have taken care of myself. If I wasn't safe walking within our territory, no one else would be either. Although, in all truthfulness, I couldn't handle myself because I was distracted by the fight with Amridon, but that wasn't the issue." She shook her head trying to clear her thoughts and stay on topic. Everything hit her so quickly it felt like she was free falling through the sky.

"The real problem was that there hadn't been an attack on a citizen in Haloti territory for thousands of years. Why would I be watching my back, or carrying concern for such an event? I wouldn't have been, and they used it against me."

She wanted to scream in anger. The more she pieced together, the more she wanted to seek revenge against the council.

"To think, on the very day of the offering I actually wished for the selection. With everything I was uncovering, it would be an easy way to escape. However, I told myself it would never happen; that this was too easy. I'd been naïve enough to think I was too important to them and look where that landed me."

The Final Offering

Grinning, she looked into his eyes, calm after getting it all out. She hadn't noticed before, but he had quite an attractive face. It was smooth and tanned, free of any imperfections. He had a squared off, powerful jaw that was becoming. "So you can see why it is easy for me to understand what you're saying. It all makes sense."

He returned her smile. "Yes, I can absolutely understand, you're just a rare find, Thula. No one has ever come to us with such an open mind before. I went through a special training so I'd be able to help you, but so far you're making this far too easy for me."

"Thanks, but it sure doesn't feel like I'm making this easy. I find it all so frustrating," she said as her eyes drifted back down.

"Who wouldn't be frustrated?" he asked. "They tore you away from everything you've ever known. And for what? Because you wised up and listened with your mind, as well as your ears. Most people don't and won't do that. That's the most intriguing aspect of all this."

Blushing, she said, "Anyway, you were doing a fine job of explaining the truth before I ran away with my little tantrum. So please, continue."

"I don't have anything else I need to tell you about our history. Normally, this would be the point where I would offer you proof, but judging by how the afternoon has gone, I don't know if it's necessary."

"Not that I need physical evidence, but what proof could you have? It's been thousands of years. Nevertheless, I have to admit I'm intrigued by what you could show me." She frowned. "It isn't a book or something, is it? A book can be easily manipulated and let's not forget something always seems to get lost in the translation. It is, after all, created by fairies."

"You're a wise woman, Thula, wiser than you know. No, it's not a book." He stood and grabbed her hands. "Come, follow me and I'll show you."

Skeptical, she rose to her feet and followed him. They wound their way down the tree and rejoined the population.

The Final Offering

Chapter 9

Thula followed Hetorian as they took a casual pace, much slower than their arrival at the secluded location. She hadn't noticed before when her emotions ran high about everything, but it felt awful hot for a late fall afternoon. Beads of moisture accumulated on her forehead and arms, with no breeze in sight.

They made their way to the lowest branch of the tree as evening neared. The biscuit she ate earlier seemed to wear off, and she noticed hunger finding its way to her stomach. As they walked, she hoped this process would be quick. She looked down at the colorful ground as they made their way across the thick branch. It was so close and it would take time to get used to it. After seventeen years of living so high in the tree, she rarely had the opportunity to see what lay beneath, but now she could look upon it anytime she wished.

They crossed halfway down the branch and she saw their destination. She understood why they had done this on the lowest branch; it was the only one wide enough to accommodate the structure.

Hidden at the base of three smaller, jutting branches was a stone structure—possibly the largest structure she had ever seen—and the first one not carved into the tree.

They stopped at the foot of a stone staircase leading to a large opening into the building.

"This, Thula, is the oldest structure anywhere on this tree. It wasn't built by the Grimmox, but rather, it was built by both of our people—the ancients. The very first settlers built this as a temple to worship God. It's not known if Grimosias or Halothias had any hand in the construction, but we know their direct children were involved." He smiled mischievously. "It's in our books."

They both laughed at the comment. She didn't know why, but she grew eager to step inside. He, unfortunately, continued talking. "This isn't a place where we worship in any one way. Everyone is free to follow their own customs. If that means praying to Halothias, by all means, do so. It's an open place of worship, just don't judge others if you see something out of the ordinary. Over time, several people worship other gods; some you've probably never even heard of."

"I understand." She nodded. "Can we enter?"

The Final Offering

"Not yet. Inside you will find two tablets. This is the proof I referred to earlier. The Haloti have their own tablets and an alarm may be ringing in your head right now, but I ask you to keep an open mind." His eyes looked pleadingly into hers.

He was right. Her skepticism had increased. The hairs on the back of her neck rose in anticipation. Tablets were no different than a book. Any skilled stoneworker could carve writing into stone. However, so far, this new friend in her life hadn't led her astray, and she agreed to reserve judgment.

He led her up the stone stairs and down an aisle. On both sides were rows of stone benches. At the far end of the building, an altar stood displaying the two stone tablets. The light cascaded through several windows lighting them up with a yellow aura.

"You'll notice the light on the tablets. This is why I wasn't in a rush to get down here. We save this part for this exact time of day so the light from the sun lights them up like this." The light danced in his eyes with the reflection of what he saw. The intensity and importance of the relic he showed her was evident. This wasn't just a building to him.

They continued their approach. Before climbing the stairs, he kissed his fingers and raised them to the sky in the same manner he had done when he had killed the caterpillar. After the gesture, they continued up the stairs.

She set her eyes on the tablets, and any questions or skepticism she had quickly drained from her mind. Somehow, she found herself weak and awestruck at the same time. Taking in the beauty sitting before her, she fell to her knees. Her heart somehow both ached and soared at the sight.

"It's breathtaking," she gasped. "I mean, we have our own tablets, but they're nothing like this. They also don't say the same thing." She paused while she read the words etched into the stone. Her misgivings vanished. "I don't understand. Who carved these?"

"No living being could have carved these. It isn't possible. Look at the curvature of the letters; the smoothness."

She did, and it was magnificent. Any stoneworker could carve words into stone, but the letters wouldn't be so smooth, so perfect. The edges were rounded, and they were all proportional to the others. It was as if God himself had created the stones around the words. "Who carved them then?"

"That can't be easily answered." A look of sorrow crossed his face. "Realizing the ruinous path we headed down as divided children of Halothias and Grimosias, we needed direction. When their father sent them back down, they brought the tablets with them. Whether the brothers created them, or if God created them, we don't know. It was never told to us and we never questioned their origin. One look is enough to realize no fairy could craft them. Have you noticed the first law?"

"I have," she nodded.

"Then read it to me. It is of the utmost importance and is how we've modeled our life."

A lump formed in her throat and she struggled to speak. "It is henceforth decreed that whether Haloti or Grimmox, we are all children of God. We are descended from the same seed and should view one another as brothers and sisters. No Haloti shall ever raise arms against the Grimmox, and no Grimmox shall ever raise arms against the Haloti; to do so will mean raising

The Final Offering

arms against God himself, and will lead to damnation for eternity outside the realm of God."

He let the words sink in. "Do you understand, Thula? Even if the Haloti attack us, which by all accounts seems to be the case, we will not fight back. You asked me earlier about our military. We have no need because God decrees it as such. Those who cause harm will be judged, and it is thus out of our hands."

"I do understand." She stopped for a moment to reflect. "Surely though, the Haloti elders know what is writ on this tablet. How then, can they expect to wage a war with the Grimmox? They would be fearful of damnation."

"That's a question we have asked ourselves. Over time, the Haloti elders have become corrupt. All they seem to care for is power, and once you have a taste, you thirst for more." He shrugged as if this explained it all. "My suspicion is that none of the Haloti elders have viewed these tablets with their own eyes. Sure the first elders viewed them thousands of years ago, but what good is it if future generations don't see it for themselves?"

"That's a good point. Why do the Grimmox get to keep the tablets for themselves?" she asked. "Wouldn't it solve a lot of our problems if allowed to visit?"

"We agree. The tablets were placed in the temple as it was the only structure that existed for worship at the time. It only made sense and involved the Haloti in the final decision. They gave their agreement to the placement. When the Haloti agreed to retreat to the upper level of the tree, we offered the temple to them. We even arranged to vacate the village so the Haloti could worship without having to ever lay eyes upon us. For the first few years, annual pilgrimages occurred where the Haloti visited. We kept our side of the bargain and cleared out, but over time, we noticed the Haloti stopped visiting. It was as if the elders finally said 'what's the point?' and gave up. We don't know the exact truth, and I doubt that even your elders would know."

She couldn't believe what she heard. Well, she could, but how could her own ancestors give up so easily? So many would have been saved if only the tradition would have continued. *How can the Grimmox be this good though?* She asked herself. It all sounded wonderful, but it seemed too good to be true. There was no reason to think he misled her in any way, but she also understood she was only getting one side of the story. She decided she would accept what he said for now, but she wasn't ready to jump in with both feet yet. It would take more time to acclimate herself and see firsthand before she committed herself to the Grimmox. Her nativity led to mistakes in the past and she vowed never to repeat them again. She needed more proof, but it wasn't yet the time.

"I thank you for all you have done for me. Am I correct in assuming this is all you had in store for me today?" she asked.

He nodded. "Yes, this is all for today."

"Good!" She smiled. "Whatever was in that biscuit did the trick, but now it has left me and I'm absolutely starving."

His eyes opened wide. "Oh my goodness, Thula, I'm so sorry. I should've thought of that sooner. Of course, you're hungry." He grabbed her arm and led her away from the temple. "I know just the place to satisfy your hunger."

The Final Offering

They walked down the stone stairs and headed back toward the main trunk of the tree. He took her to the winding staircase, and they set out in search of the only thing that could quench the churning beasts inside their stomachs.

The Final Offering

Chapter 10

She rolled over in her bed as rays of sunlight crept through her window. Her back was sore, and she thought it would be a long day. The first night in her new home had been less than ideal; she tossed and turned all night to get comfortable. As she lay in bed now, it was a losing battle and she chose instead to get up.

Nature came to life all around her as she walked out and strolled down the branch. Several crows fought over the carcass of a dead squirrel out on the plains. She took a seat and breathed in the damp, sweet morning air.

"Thula, is that you?" A voice spoke to her.

She turned and looked. It was another female Haloti, and she stared long and hard, trying to put the face with a name. "Charlonne?" Charlonne was the offering five years before. They were the same age and had even played as children.

A wide smile broached Charlonne's face. "Yes, I admit I'm rather surprised myself." She ran around the bench, dropping the cloth she carried as she wrapped her hands around her old friend.

Thula returned the warm hug. "Charlonne, I forgot you had been taken."

Mock sadness filled Charlonne's face and eyes. "I thought we were closer than that. I'm only kidding. I remember how it was. When they take someone away, we tend to brush them with our minds. It's the only way we could cope. We were young anyway."

"You have no idea how nice it is to see a familiar face." She pulled Charlonne down on the bench with her.

"How have you been?" she realized her mistake. "Other than being brought down here, that is." Thula saw a sheepish look cross her friend's face.

"Yeah, I've been good. Coming here was a blessing in disguise." Charlonne looked on with concern. Thula took a deep breath and continued, "I've had an interesting year…" She told her old friend all about the events leading to her selection as the offering.

"I'm at a loss, Thula. I'm so sorry you had to go through so many trials." She patted Thula's hand in a consoling manner.

The Final Offering

"It's okay. At least I'm starting to put everything together." She smiled as she leaned in a little closer. "You've been here for five years, how have you adjusted? Do you feel betrayed by the elders?"

Charlonne sighed. "It wasn't easy at first; my age played a factor in that. But everyone here is so friendly and warm. Once I got over the sadness of leaving my family behind, I acclimated to my new life. I don't feel betrayed by the elders in as much as I'm free now and at peace for the first time in my life."

Thula nodded. "But did you buy right into what they told you? I mean, how long did it take you to accept everything?"

"Well, it was hard. In fact, I held a lot of resentment toward the Grimmox for a long time. I blamed them for pulling me away from my family. As I've grown older, I've come to see the truth." She stood and walked a little way down the branch, but turned at the last minute. "If you're struggling with the facts, don't. Can't you see how it all makes sense?"

Thula stood and walked closer to Charlonne. "No, that's just it. Of course, it makes sense. Especially after everything I went through in the program. It makes complete sense." She saw the smile grow on Charlonne's face. "It's just that... I don't know. I trust everything Hetorian told me, I really do, but it all seems too good like it's too easy. I don't know, I mean, how can the Haloti have so much hate, while the Grimmox offer nothing but love? It makes me feel hatred toward God for making me a Haloti." Knowing she must sound like an immature child to her old friend, she twisted her hands in her lap.

"I've wondered the same thing. It made me uncomfortable like I was being brainwashed all over again. But it's not like that, though. The hall of records is open to all of us, and you're welcome to spend as much time down there as you like. What Hetorian told you was only a brief glance. In the hall, they have archives depicting the full history of the Grimmox. They're not as harmless or innocent as he has described. In fact, the original battle with the Haloti started by an advancement by the Grimmox."

"Then why didn't Hetorian say that?" she asked. Her eyes darkened like an oncoming storm.

"That's part of the next phase. I'm sure Hetorian will get to that soon. It's not as if he withheld it, they just have a process they follow. You'll see." Charlonne put her hand on Thula's shoulder, at once offering comfort and familiarity.

"I hope so. It would make me feel better about everything."

Thula wanted to shift the conversation and not waste this chance to catch up. "So tell me, how is your life?"

"It's good. I was sealed last year to the love of my life, a Grimmox named Bermiel. In fact," she patted her stomach, "we're expecting our first child. We still have a long way to go, it's early, but we're both very excited."

"Congratulations, that's so exciting." Thula jumped up and hugged her friend.

"Thanks," Charlonne said. She looked over Thula's shoulder. "Look, it's been great catching up and I can't wait to discuss things further with you, but now isn't the time, I've actually got to get this cloth down to the factory. But I'm

The Final Offering

warmed by your presence. If you have questions, seek me out. I live on the fourth level and anyone can point you in my direction." They hugged again before she picked up the cloth and made her way down the branch.

Thula watched her leave rather abruptly, thankful to have a friend. As Charlonne disappeared, she thought she understood the reason behind the quick departure. She saw Hetorian making his way over in her direction, another lesson to begin.

The Final Offering

Chapter 11

Thula sat alone on the bench in the middle of the common area. Alone with her thoughts, she wondered what the day would have in store. She didn't know why, but she couldn't seem to get Hetorian's face out of her head. He was quite possibly the most beautiful man she had ever seen. Was she falling in love with him already? She hoped not. Everything happened too quickly. But still, ever since she first laid her eyes upon him, as he hunted the caterpillar, there had been something about him; a quality she found fascinating, and it set her stomach aflutter. Someone approaching from behind her, and she snapped out of her dreamy trance.

"Good morning. I hope you slept well." He looked around. "Judging by how early you're out and about, I would assume you did not."

Somehow, it was reassuring to be back in his presence and she smiled. It felt comforting, the way Amridon used to make her feel. "Unfortunately, I'm sad to report I tossed and turned all night." She shrugged and offered a slight smile.

"I'm sorry to hear that. I came down to see if you wanted to grab breakfast before we begin," he said.

"Come to think of it, I am hungry. Is there any way we can begin while we eat breakfast?" she asked. She wanted him to know she was eager to get things underway.

"Of course! You're the boss. Let's go down to the second branch. There is a pastry shop that makes the sweetest biscuits you've ever tasted."

She followed his lead. They arrived in front of a door that looked like all the other doors in the tree. There was no sign or any other marking to show it as a bakery. This was curious to Thula, and she furrowed her brow trying to figure out why.

He opened the door and led her inside. Immediately the aroma of spiced cakes, baked pastries, warmed bread, and the like assaulted her senses. They selected a table by the window where they could look out upon the village. "I didn't see a sign, how is one to know this is a bakery?"

"You'll come to figure it all out. Since everything is owned by the village, there is no need for any signage. We have two bakeries serving us; this one and one on the fifth branch."

The Final Offering

"Interesting," she said. "So what's in store for me today?" she asked as she slid back in her chair.

"I'm afraid that after our discussions yesterday, you may think I'm painting the Haloti in a negative light. I want you to know that's not the case. The Grimmox have plenty mistakes in our long history too. In fact, we started the feud that started the long war, resulting in the return of Grimosias and Halothias to the living world. It's possibly the worst moment in our long history, and we are very saddened by the deaths caused by it."

"I understand. I was also told your history is recorded in the hall of records and I could visit it at any time." She said her words matter-of-factly.

Perplexed, Hetorian said, "Yes. That's correct. How did you find out about the hall?" he asked.

"I ran into Charlonne before you showed up. I asked her about everything I learned yesterday."

"Ah, yes, Charlonne. You are both about the same age if I'm not mistaken. Did you know each other as children?" he asked.

She nodded yes. "We played together many times when we were little."

"So you were checking up on me? Making sure the information I gave you was correct?" he asked. His eyes rested on hers... she wasn't sure if he was reassuring or challenging?

"Well, no. Believing you wasn't the issue. I had a hunch it all sounded too good to be true. Or at least that things were missing. It all seemed too perfect as if you were painting a picture of Grimmox good, Haloti bad. I needed to hear from someone else in my position to understand what it all meant. And there she was."

"I see," he replied. "So are you satisfied now?"

She chuckled. "No, not yet. I'm still trying to come to terms with what you've told me. What was the tipping point? I mean, how did it all change for you?"

"I won't lie, it took time. We hated the Haloti just as much as they hated us. And even after the sons of God visited, it took time to get over the animosity. There were many, especially the older Grimmox, who thought we should ignore the tablets and seek retribution for the deaths they caused once our numbers returned to a more stable level, but over time those changed." His gaze shifted down as though he were gathering his next thoughts.

"Yes, but how?" she asked. "I'm really interested. I have so much anger, so much resentment towards them myself, and they're my people. How did the Grimmox come to terms with it so easily?"

He sat and pondered for a moment. "There is no hard and fast reason why everything changed. As the older population died, new blood that had no experience with the Haloti took its place. We studied the tablets and meditated on their meaning." He gestured with his hands. She could see his full heart was in his explanation.

"We disbanded our military to take away any wish to conquer and moved toward a more peaceful society. It has worked well thus far."

The Final Offering

"But why did you adopt a peaceful attitude while the Haloti continued their hateful stance? I don't know all the details, but I would assume once the Grimmox went toward peace, the Haloti would have done the same."

"I don't have an answer for that, but as I said yesterday, it's because we had the tablets, you did not. I don't know if this explains everything. I mean, the Grimmox were still plotting revenge too, we're just fortunate that future generations saw the truth and dedicated their lives to peace."

"The Haloti are about to go too far," she said, shifting her gaze to penetrate his. "An attack is imminent. If not this winter, I would say by the spring at the latest. What are we going to do to prepare?"

His gaze was just as penetrating as he took a deep breath and said, "We'll do nothing. We're not going to live in fear, nor will we raise the military. We vowed not to lift arms against our brothers and sisters, so if death is what God has in store for us, then so be it." His bearing was calm, serene even.

Thula's face turned angry. "I can't just sit back and wait to die. I already paid the ultimate sacrifice, I'm not about to do it again."

"What will you do then?" he asked. His demeanor remained easy. "If the council gets word that there is the potential you will use weapons against the Haloti, I'm afraid you will be forced to leave our village too. You need to pray and meditate to find the answers you seek. If it so happens, you receive a message guiding you to fight, then so be it, but otherwise, we are given to peace at all costs." He laid his arms on her shoulders to cool her rising ire.

"I'm not talking about fighting my own people, I just want you to defend yourselves," her voice rose as her anger increased. "And you can't pray to solve everything. God listens, this much I understand, but if you only do as you believe he wishes, you will miss out on a lot in life. Sometimes you need to step out and risk it."

She shook her head in frustration. Obviously, she wasn't getting through to him.

"I understand your stance, and can see the point about peace, but there are peaceful ways to end this before it even begins."

Hetorian sighed. "What exactly would you suggest?" he asked.

"For starters, why don't we send an emissary, or a group of people to have a discussion with the Haloti elders? It's not the best method, but we need to start somewhere, don't we?"

"That option has been considered ever since we caught word of their new plans. The council thought it over and determined based on experience, we would be wasting our time, as it would only create more issues."

She exhaled sharply, "Okay, what if we gathered a group of ex-Haloti and snuck into the village? Couldn't we try to talk to the people? I'm sure if we could get through to some, we could bring at least a couple of them down here to see the tablets. All it would take is a few, and they could start a revolt amongst the population."

"I'm afraid it would be too dangerous." He paused, as he considered his words. "First, you would need to actually

The Final Offering

convince the offerings to undertake this mission. I'm sure if you talked to enough of them, you would learn many of them would never do this. They left that life behind many years ago and would rather die than go back to their homeland. Secondly, you would never get that far. The guards have orders to kill any Haloti who may try to return. Think about it for a moment. If you were to return, don't you think it would create an uproar amongst the Haloti people? There would be chaos and there would be attempts to depose the elder's positions, at the very least." He offered a consolatory smile. "We've been through all the different scenarios and there doesn't appear to be a peaceful resolution."

"I can't accept that. I won't accept that. There is always an answer. We just have to find it." Her anger increased again.

He leaned forward and grasped her hands in his own. "But you have to, Thula. There is no other way."

She pulled her hands back. "I don't buy it." She got up and stared out at the surrounding branches as if she would find their answer among the foliage.

He shook his head in frustration. "So be it. That's your choice and I won't stand in the way. Will you at least listen to everything I say over the next week before you jump to any rash decisions? Listen, and if you still feel the same way, I'll go with you to the council and support your decision."

She thought about it for a moment. "I guess haven't told me everything yet. I'll agree to your wishes but will hold you to your promise. If I feel the same way at the end of the week, I expect you to go with me. I'm sure I'll need the support."

"Very well," he nodded. "Shall we continue then?"

J.G. Gatewood

She nodded and listened intently. After breakfast, they left the bakery and headed up to the secluded spot where they spoke the previous day. He continued describing the past and the customs of the Grimmox people.

The Final Offering

Chapter 12

After four more days of information, Hetorian arranged for her to meet several more of the former Haloti. It was a cooler afternoon, and she even smelled a hint of snow in the air. They gathered in Charlonne's home, and it didn't surprise her to see several familiar faces. She had already grown comfortable as a part of Grimmox society, but she still held on to her Haloti ways as she tried to reconcile the two with each other. It was helpful to be in the company of so many old friends.

After the beginning pleasantries, many inquired what was happening in their old home. She described her previous months, much to the dismay of those in attendance. But the overwhelming theme was they were glad they were no longer a part of that old way of life. When she described the impending attack, her heart sank when they all adopted the same reasoning as Hetorian.

She asked if any would go back with her, and just as Hetorian predicted, none of them agreed.

"We have to do something. We can't sit back and wait for our deaths," she said.

One of her new friends spoke up. "But don't you see it would go against everything we believe in?"

"So you're all ready to embrace your own end?" she asked. "You, of all people, should understand the need to do something. They took you from your homes, forced you to start a new life in a place they told you was dangerous and awful. You're willing to allow them to take what little you have created for yourselves here? Just like that." She snapped her fingers and glared around the room.

Charlonne, who had remained quiet thus far, spoke up. "Don't you see? We are doing something, we have faith God will take care of us. This isn't the first time the Haloti have tried something like this, but something always thwarted their attempts. We have to trust we will be protected again. That everything will work out."

"How can you have so much faith?" she asked as she looked at each of them in turn, challenging them. "What about all your children? Don't you care about their futures?"

"Of course we do. You can ask any of them who are old enough to respond, and I'm sure they will tell you they would much rather die."

The Final Offering

Thula's heart sank; she couldn't find the words to describe her thoughts. Gazing around the room, she looked at those in attendance and said, "So, I guess I should just get used to the idea then; wait for my death."

"It doesn't have to be that sad. We won't sit back idly while we wait for our deaths. We'll embrace the time we have. You should do the same." The young girl smiled at Thula.

Leaving Charlonne's home, she felt dejected. They adopted a laissez-faire attitude, and she hated it. She needed time to work out her thoughts so she could come up with an actionable plan that would convince the Grimmox to defend themselves. With no clear destination in mind, she looked around at her surroundings. There was nothing needing her attention in her quarters and with nowhere else to go, she walked to Hetorian's home. He let her in and brought her to his couch.

"What's wrong, Thula? I expected you to come back happy after seeing so many of your old friends. It should be a joyful day, but all I see in your eyes is deep sadness. Tell me what happened."

Tears welled up in the corners of her eyes. "It went exactly as you expected. I brought up doing something to stop the Haloti, but they all shared your sentiments. They refuse to do anything." She rested her head on his shoulder.

"I'm sorry. I figured this would happen, but you have to understand this is as it must be. It's what Grimosias decreed. You shouldn't have expected anything less. If their beliefs were wishy-washy and quick to change, they wouldn't count for much, would they?"

Brushing away the tears, she looked up at his face. "I suppose you're right." She sighed. "So now what?"

"We'll finish your acclimation program. Whatever happens after that is up to you."

She stared at him for several moments, unable to find suitable words to describe her emotions. More than anything, she was infuriated. Somehow, she had escaped the icy tentacles of the Haloti elders who wished her dead, only to come to the Grimmox who refused to do anything to protect themselves. Even here, where she should be safe, she still faced the possibility of death. She hated her life and the role she had taken in bringing this all about.

A burning filler her stomach and she wanted to cry, to scream, to show any emotion. Hetorian's warm face brought her comfort as her emotions warred like ferocious animals within her. His smile and bright eyes invited her in, calming her spirit. Without understanding why she leaned forward and kissed him. At first, he seemed hesitant, but he relaxed and ran his pale hands up the dark skin of her arms.

A shiver ran up her spine, raising the hairs on her back and arms. His lips were soft, and she yearned for more as he pulled her in closer. He ran his hands up to brush the nape of her neck. The kiss was passionate, much more than her first kiss with Amridon. That kiss had felt good; this kiss was amazing. She ran her fingers through his soft hair. His breath tasted sweet, but she got a hint of spice too. Her animalistic instincts took over, and she bit his lower lip. Not hard enough to cause pain or bring out blood, but in a friendly, playful way. He responded by increasing the vigor and voracity of his own kisses as he grabbed the back of her head and brought her in closer.

The Final Offering

He turned her head and nibbled on her earlobe, softly caressing it with his lips. It brought out more shivers in her body, and she squirmed.

She rubbed her hand gently on his thigh. His muscles stiffened, and he pushed her back.

"Thula," she chased him and planted her lips on his, but he again pulled back. "Thula, we can't do this."

He was right. It didn't make it any better, but she understood his hesitation. "I know." She smiled. "Thanks though, I needed that."

"You and me both," he smirked. "It might surprise you to hear this, but I've never kissed anyone before."

"What?" she gasped. "How can that be possible?"

"I don't know." He looked sullen. "I guess I was just waiting for the right person. When you leaned forward, it felt meant to be."

"Well, I'm not one to talk. I've only kissed one other person, and he was the love of my life, but I soon found out otherwise."

"Come here," he said. He pulled her in closer and they sat on the couch in companionable silence. Just enjoying each other's company, both lost in thought.

"So, how do we move ahead?" she asked. "I mean, what should I do?"

"I'm not sure I can answer that question for you. I've never been in your position before, and you need to follow your heart."

"That's just it," she said. "My heart seems torn. I don't know what's best, but I have to do something; even if it means attacking my own kind."

"I've told you how I feel about it," he frowned. "I cannot participate should the Haloti wage a war."

"Not that I agree with you, but I understand just the same." She looked up into his eyes. "Maybe it's up to me to try to talk sense into them. I doubt it—especially considering how the elders viewed me when they sent me away—but I can try, can't I?"

"Hopefully it will never come to that," he said as he pulled her in closer.

The Final Offering

Chapter 13

Thula sat on the edge of her bed as she prepared for the day. The wind outside howled as it flew around the trunk of the tree. Winter would be upon them soon, evident by the biting cold the wind out of the northwest brought in. All leaves had fallen from the tree, and it sat empty and naked—a brown skeleton, stark against the blue, cloudless sky. It wouldn't be long before a pillowy, white blanket of snow covered the ground.

Over the previous days, she had had a lot of time to reflect. Hetorian had gone over everything, and in a few days, there would be a celebration to welcome her as one of the Grimmox.

Although she had learned everything, she still didn't feel as though she were a part of them. But, not with the Haloti either. She guessed she probably never would fit in either place now.

To help guide her on her path and acclimation into her new society, Hetorian had repeatedly asked her to spend time in the temple in meditation. He mentioned this could very well be the only path she had to find the answers she sought. The idea wasn't a comfortable prospect for her at first—never having been religious before—but having found answers nowhere else it seemed like the only way.

As she pulled on her clothes, her stomach grumbled. In preparation for her trip to the temple, Hetorian suggested she fast for two days. He said it was the only way to clear one's mind and prepare the body for deep meditation. All she wanted to do, though, was eat.

Just the thought of him brought a small smile to her lips as she reluctantly pulled her shirt over her shoulders and wings before grabbing a cloak to protect her from the whipping wind.

She stepped out on the branch and looked to the west. Foreboding, gray clouds filled the horizon, ready to unleash the full fury of their pent-up anger. Wrapping the cloak closer around her chest to ward off the reaching tendrils of wind, she walked down to the bottom branch. The temple sat farther ahead, filling her view and sitting like a monument in the distance.

Polished, white stairs greeted her as she reached the temple and began the climb—trepidation filled her body. Each step became more difficult, and she felt immoral; as though she walked toward the beginning of the end. She pushed on and

The Final Offering

finally reached the top where the open doors welcomed her like the warm embrace of a relative.

The instant heat offered by the many braziers lit throughout, filled the room with a dim, orange, flickering glow as she walked in. A member of the clergy stood just inside in flowing black robes stretching to the floor.

"Thula, welcome to the temple." He bowed gracefully. "My name is Netharian. Hetorian informed me of your intent."

"Thank you, Netharian." She wasn't sure what to do and returned the bow.

"We've prepared a private room for your meditation. Every person experiences it differently, and we never know quite how long it will take, so we find a private room to be the most suitable." He turned. "If you would please follow me."

He led her down the aisle toward the rear of the temple. She watched him, and it didn't appear he walked at all. It looked more like a glide; his body seemed to float in front of her. Taking her past the altar with the tablets, they approached a door on the left. He pushed it open and motioned for her to enter.

The stone room looked plain with white walls and a single window. Several pillows were arranged on the floor and a single brazier sat in the middle.

She turned to Netharian. "Thank you. This will suit me just fine," she smiled.

"If there's anything else you need I'll either be in the sanctuary or my office, right across the hall. Don't hesitate to come find me." He disappeared and closed the door behind him.

She walked around the room as she examined her surroundings. With the door closed, the heat in the tiny room increased rapidly. Feeling the sweat form on her forehead, she took off her cloak before she dripped with sweat.

Standing in front of the pillows, she dropped to her knees. With no idea how to begin, she looked around at her surroundings. The wind rattled the window as the storm picked up outside, and the hunger pains in her stomach intensified.

She brought her hands together and closed her eyes. "Lord, God, Grimosias or Halothias, whoever may be listening, it's me, Thula. I'm sure you know what I'm trying to do, but I've come to you for help," she whispered. "I'm trying to come to terms with my new home, but I seem to be at a crossroads. Whatever you can do to help, to show me what I'm supposed to do, would be appreciated."

With nothing else to say, she opened her eyes and gazed about the room. She didn't know what to expect, but the room remained silent. Sighing, she closed her eyes again.

Maybe it's my fault, she thought. *If I never would've joined the program, none of this would be happening. I'm sure the elders would still be working on their plan, but I basically handed it to them.*

Who am I kidding? She laughed. *They would have found someone else to use as a pawn. The Haloti are filled with individuals willing to blindly follow whatever it is the elders speak.*

The Final Offering

Her thoughts drifted to Amridon. *How did it all go so wrong? I thought we were meant for each other, we even approached our parents to begin a courtship. How did the elders brainwash him to the point he would forego our relationship?* When he had spoken to her, he hadn't sounded like himself. It was as though they were speaking to her, through him. It wasn't him at all. She wanted to know how they had done it, but couldn't figure it out. After all, if they could do it with Amridon, who else in the Haloti had they manipulated in such a manner.

Her shirt stuck to her back and her hair clung in strings to her face. The room had warmed up so much, the sweat dripped off her body in a constant flow. Drops trickled down her back and tickled her, making her squirm. A lightheadedness tickled her mind. Too much longer in the sweltering heat and she thought, she might just pass out.

"Come on! If you're going to speak to me, do it now. My patience wears thin." She said.

She looked around the room again, but everything remained the same. Raindrops fell outside and pelted the window. It was cold enough outside she thought it might turn to sleet before too long, and when that happened, the branches would become treacherous.

In anger, she stood, deciding enough was enough. She turned to the door to leave as her vision blurred. At first, she thought it was the sweat and reached up to brush it away from her eyes. She soon realized it wasn't the sweat blurring her vision; her energy waned. Struggling, she tried to take a step forward and fell to her knees. Taking a deep breath, she tried to control herself, but she needed to get help. On wobbly knees, she stood, took another breath and tried to step forward. She reached forward with her hand and missed the doorknob, falling backward and hitting her head on the stone floor.

The Final Offering

Chapter 14

Thula walked along one of the upper branches of the Haloti territory. The sun beat down on her face, but she didn't mind. She noticed the new, bright green leaves had come in, signaling the end of spring and the beginning of summer. Brushed her hands across the tips of the leaves, she strolled along. It felt good on her palms, almost tickling them. She didn't know where she was going, and in reality, she didn't really care.

She walked toward the end of the branch and stared down, far below her the first signs of life made their presence known. The tips of the first sprouts showed lime green as they pierced the thick, black dirt of the ground, still wet with moisture from last night's storms. The beauty of nature surrounding her, and she marveled at how far they had come as a species.

A tickling in the back of her mind, like a distant dream or whisper, garnered her attention. She rubbed her head with the palm of her hand and discovered a large knot on the back. Suddenly, pain ripped through her head, throbbing pain as if someone had hit her with a hammer. She couldn't remember doing anything to create this injury, but realization dawned on her face. *I hit my head on the ground,* she remembered.

Blinked her eyes and staring at the blank walls of the room, her vision cleared as the hallucination disappeared before her eyes. The piles of blankets sat just inches away from where her head rested. She tasted the warm, earthy aroma of blood collecting in her mouth. She must have bit her tongue when she fell, or from the collision with the hard ground.

Sitting up, she tried to blink away the pain, although all attempts seemed futile. She stood on her still shaky legs and tried to regain her balance. Taking a breath, she stepped forward when the room grew blurry yet again. *I need to get out of here,* she thought. The wall appeared to melt away, like water flowing down the smooth glass of a window. Everything around her dropped to the ground, and she saw herself surrounded by pure white. Using her hands, she hid her eyes to ward off the sudden brightness, and the pounding in her head as it intensified. When they adjusted to the light, she looked around and saw two figures standing before her.

Man, I must have really done a number on my head, she thought. *These hallucinations are so real.*

The Final Offering

One of the figures spoke. "That's because it is real." The figure smiled as the other spoke.

"And yes, you hit your head hard, but it's nothing that won't heal up, in time."

The pair strode toward her. She grimaced assuming these were more hallucinations and took a couple steps back in fear.

"There's nothing to be afraid of, Thula. This is what you came here for," the first figure said.

"Came where for? This is why they chose me as the offering?" she asked.

The pair looked at one another and laughed. The second figure spoke. "In a sense, yes. You are the exact vessel we need to put an end to this madness, but no. That's not what I was referring to. What I meant was this is what you came here for. The reason you turned to meditation."

She realized this wasn't a hallucination after all. "Came here? Meditation? Who exactly are you?" she asked, rubbing her head gingerly where she had hit it.

"Thula, we are the sons of your creator." He looked at the other. "This is Grimosias, and my name is Halothias." A smile filled both of their faces. They both wore long flowing, colorful robes, but looked just like any other of their race. Thula could see the resemblance.

She still couldn't grasp what was happening to her. "But how?" she asked. "I don't understand. You're both long dead, generations, even millennia ago. How could you stand here before me?"

"We're not standing before you, in the normal sense of speaking. But, we are communicating with you. Currently, you lay unconscious in the meditation room you were using." Halothias pointed to the floor to her right. "Take a look for yourself."

She turned her head as the floor suddenly shimmered back into existence. Sure enough, her body lay, as if dead, in a heap on the floor. "But how is this possible?"

"Our father sent us down here to *chat* with you," Grimosias said and grinned a goofy smile. "We needed an opportunity, and you finally provided us with one."

Grimosias had long, white hair with a smooth, light-colored face. He stood a little taller and thinner than his brother, Halothias, who had shorter, dark hair, but the same ageless face. She walked forward and touched the hand of Halothias, just to make sure it was real. The soft flesh responded to her touch, and she jumped back. "So I'm not hallucinating?" she asked.

"I'm afraid this is all real, just in a different realm than where you normally reside." Again they both giggled in a somehow boyish way. Thula thought she could find it endearing if she wasn't half unconscious and confused.

"But Halothias," she realized whom she was addressing, "I'm sorry, can I call you that?" He nodded. "Halothias, your skin is light. All the Haloti are dark skinned. We always assumed you were too. That's how you are in all of your paintings, anyway."

"I'm not what you expected then?" He asked. "We were both born to the same father, in his image, if you will. Why would he make one of us dark skinned while the other had pale

The Final Offering

skin?" he paused while she thought it over. "Evolution, Thula. The Haloti moved to the uppermost part of the tree. There is less leaf cover at the top to offer shade. Your ancestors suffered periods of severe burns, and as a result, the Haloti skin has grown to adapt over time, becoming darker in color." A grin formed on his lips. "That doesn't take anything away from you, though. You're the same regardless of your skin, aren't you?"

She suddenly had so many questions she needed answers to but decided she needed to start with her main concern. "What am I supposed to do? I assume you know all about the current state of our two races."

Grimosias stepped forward. "We're very concerned and it is the whole reason we have come down to our children for only the second time since our deaths." She kept rubbing the knot on the back of her head with her hand. "Let me take care of that."

He walked forward and ran his hand over the troublesome spot. "That should help." He smiled. "Does it feel better?"

She rubbed her head and found only the smoothness of her scalp. Her eyes grew wide. It was gone as if he had tapped her with an invisible wand. "That's amazing. Thank you."

"It was the least my brother could do for you," Halothias said. He poked him with his elbow as brothers are known to do. "You must have many worries. Where would you like to begin?"

"How about the beginning? I want to know the truth."

They looked at each other and sighed. "All right, Thula. This may not be a short conversation, so I urge you to get comfortable."

She nodded as a chair materialized behind her out of thin air, almost forcing her to sit. The pair as they looked at one another, deciding who should go first.

The Final Offering

Chapter 15

Grimosias strode forward in the white emptiness surrounding them. His footfalls made no sound as he stepped closer. "Much of what you've Hetorian told you is the truth, although it twisted over time, as most things will." He shared a smirk with his brother.

Halothias joined him as they came toward her. Two more chairs materialized—just a few feet in front of her and they both gracefully sank into them.

Grimosias continued. "It is true all of our children were near extinction at their own hands. Centuries of brutal war dwindled them to nothingness. Our father thought it best if both sides obliterated one another. That way, he could start over, with a blank slate, so to speak. At our urging, he agreed to let us come down, to correct our mistakes, and redirect our children."

Halothias spoke, and she turned her head to follow his words. It grew difficult to keep up as they switched speakers. "They didn't accept us at first; it took convincing to put an end to the war. We found it difficult for the living mind to comprehend our physical forms and we never visited again."

"And it's why we approached you in the manner we have today," Grimosias added.

"Yes, we thought it best for you to find us in your own way; that it would be easier for you to deal with and comprehend. After years of deliberation, we finally got both sides to throw down their weapons, and they agreed to no further attacks. We worked with them to get both sides—Grimmox and Haloti alike—to realize they were brothers and sisters and they were hurting only themselves."

"We urged them to throw away our old feuds, to live in peace, but it didn't seem possible," Grimosias said. "We decided there was no way to get them to come together, but we got them to agree to never raise a weapon against one another."

"That's when we created the tablets. We figured if it were in writing, there would be no way we would ever see a war between the two again. We made it the first law in the hopes it would dissuade any further aggression."

"It worked well for several generations," Grimosias said. "Both sides kept their distance, and both visited the temple for frequent services," he smiled. "Yes, it seemed we had done everything right. But we were wrong."

The Final Offering

"The Haloti's visits became further and further apart. It seemed two elders rose to power among them intent on seeing themselves placed above the Grimmox through any means necessary. While they understood it would never happen in their lifetime, they hoped for it to hold among future generations," Halothias said.

"No longer visiting the temple, they lost their direction over time and looked to only the elders for guidance," Grimosias said with sadness creeping across his face.

"Yes, the Haloti lost their way. It took many centuries to reach the point they have today, but it's not what we set forth for them." The same sadness creased Halothias' features.

"Maybe if you would've forgone your 'we are gods too belief', we wouldn't be in this position right now," Grimosias said to his brother.

"Are we not immortal? Have we not proven that by coming down here today?" Halothias questioned his brother hotly. "If today's acts aren't enough proof, I don't know what is."

"That's not the point, *brother,*" Grimosias said with sarcasm dripping from his tongue. "We may be of God, but we are not gods in our own right. I would've thought you'd have learned this by now." Grimosias rolled his eyes.

Thula couldn't understand what transpired. It seemed some things never changed; at least if you believed the stories of their older days.

"This is getting us nowhere. You'd think we would've solved this by now," Halothias said, rolling his eyes in turn.

Grimosias took a moment to compose himself. "Yes, you're correct." He turned back to Thula. "While the elders controlled the Haloti, and molded them to fit their ideal of what should happen, the Grimmox followed the tablets but took it to the extreme. Not only have they thrown down their weapons, they refuse to even stand up for themselves. As a sentient being, they should never expect to sit back and wait for death. That's not what our Father wants either."

"The point being, neither side is right. We want you to coexist peacefully, but are you always going to get along?" Halothias asked. "Of course not. We expected the occasional squabble," he grinned. "You saw with your own eyes that my brother and I still can't agree with each other on everything. But the difference is we don't destroy one another."

"Yes, we argue, yes we get into tiffs, but we work it out verbally." Grimosias looked in Halothias' direction. "If he were ever to raise a sword against me, I would do the same. I must! To defend myself, would I kill him? No, nor would he kill me. We would work it out, or agree to disagree."

They both paused and Thula took a moment to reflect. "So you want us to fight?" she asked.

Grimosias frowned. "I thought you were smarter than that, Thula. No, we don't *want* you to fight, but if the Haloti raise their weapons, we expect the Grimmox to meet them head-on. One side must force the other to the table to open discussions and work out your differences."

"We're running out of time. We're not here on behalf of our Father. He seems content to let this play out as it may. If the

The Final Offering

Haloti destroy the Grimmox, Father will wipe the Haloti from the face of the planet as a punishment," Halothias said.

"Nor would he allow the Grimmox into the next life either. He will not accept an entire race of martyrs into his kingdom," Grimosias added.

"You have to get both sides to agree. The Grimmox need to raise up their weapons and meet the threat on the field of battle, then you must convince the Haloti to throw down their own. Only then can you work on a peaceful resolution," Halothias said somberly.

"Even if I could convince the Haloti soldiers to do as you instructed, how do you expect me to convince the elders? They won't easily succumb as they more than likely already know the truth," Thula said. She looked at them both with intensity and questions burning in her eyes.

"We never said it would be easy," Halothias said. "You have to have faith and hope it all works out. We'll be watching, and if there is anything we can do, we will."

"You've come before me, can't you come forward to everyone else too?" she asked.

"Have you been listening? It isn't that easy. I'm afraid our Father would never stand for it," Grimosias said. "We can speak to one—such as yourself—and He won't notice, but to present ourselves to everyone would go against his decree to not mettle in mortals' lives."

"I'm afraid his vengeance would be too great if we did. He might kill you all as a punishment for our actions," Halothias said.

"We're counting on you," Grimosias said with a smile. "The existence of our entire population depends on your success. Not to put any pressure on you or anything." He winked at her.

"You'll be just fine, Thula. Your instincts have served you well thus far. I'm sure they will continue to guide you going forward." Halothias put his arm on her shoulder.

"I don't know if I can do it," she said, her shoulders sagging with the weight of it all.

"You're our last hope," they both said in unison. "We know you can handle it."

"Our time draws nigh and now it will be up to you," Grimosias added. "Follow your heart, and we thank you for what you're doing."

Thula rose to her feet. "But wait, how can I do...." She fell over as her spirit blended back into her body.

The Final Offering

Chapter 16

Thula opened her eyes and stared at the blank, empty walls. The heat from the brazier hit her like a brick and her clothes were damp with sweat. She stood up and looked around. *A dream,* she thought. *It was only a dream.*

It sure hadn't felt like a dream, but then again she was starving. She opened the door to the room and walked out into the temple. The change in temperature was a great blessing. All was silent, and she didn't see anyone inside. Walking out the doors of the temple, she crept down the stone stairs. *Wait,* she thought, *if that was a dream, shouldn't I have a knot on my head? And shouldn't it be pounding?*

She reached the back of her head and her skull felt smooth. A tingle ran up her spine and she stopped dead in her tracks. "It wasn't a dream, they contacted me," she said.

Suddenly, she didn't know what to do, and she thought about everything they told her. Thoughts raced through her mind as she tried to come up with a plan. Her eyes darted from side to side as she looked around the village. *Hetorian,* she thought, *he'll know what to do.* At least she hoped he would help her craft a plan.

Without another thought, she took off running and hit the stairs. She climbed up two levels and ran straight toward his house as screams filled the air.

Farther down the branch, she heard a voice. "The Haloti are here! The end draws near!" Commotion filled the town square below as people scrambled to find their loved ones. The Haloti were already making their move. She had thought they'd have months or at least weeks to plan, but it looked like she would have to speed up the process and put something into motion today. It didn't leave her much time.

With increased vigor, she continued to Hetorian's home. She pounded on the door and tried to wait. After a long moment, the door cracked open, and he peered out at her through his bright green eyes. His wings twitched in nervous anticipation. "Thula, what is it?" He seemed surprised by her sudden appearance as he looked around the village, then back to her. "What happened to you? What's going on? Shouldn't you be in the temple?" he asked.

The Final Offering

A bell tolled three times from below and his eyes lit up.

"I don't have much time, Hetorian. It appears the Haloti have arrived, and I would assume they're not here on friendly terms," she said. "Grab your bow and let's go."

"Thula, I've already told you I won't fight against them, and neither will anyone else," he protested, face set.

"I don't have time to explain myself right now; I'll do it on the way. Just grab your bow and let's go." She urged. He looked at her with a blank stare. "I had a revelation during my time at the temple. Now hurry!"

His eyes widened, and he ran into his home, grabbing his bow as she instructed, before running back out to meet her. "Okay, I did as you said. Now tell me what's going on."

"On the way, let's go." She turned and stormed off. He had a hard time keeping up with her. "Tell the others to grab their weapons."

"Thula, I know what you're trying to do and it won't work," he said grimly.

"If my plan works, you won't need to use them," she said, sounding resolute.

"So what, it's all just a ploy? A tactic to get them to back off?" he asked.

"Yes." She realized she didn't have a weapon herself. "Is there somewhere I can get a bow? I'll need something."

"Yes, the hunting armory is up one level. I assume we're going up anyway, so we can stop there and get what we need," he sounded winded.

"Very well." Her voice sounded calm and smooth. "Keep telling everyone until we get up there."

They spread the word as they worked their way up the tree. She could see the panic and hesitation on each of their faces. They would never arm themselves at her word, but coming from Hetorian, they all did as he said. It seemed they were well versed in following his instructions.

They reached the next level, and he pointed to the door. She ran up to it and demanded a bow and quiver. The clerk inside looked uncertain at first but saw Hetorian and several others armed and waiting for her. He quickly gave her what she sought. She ordered him to arm himself and join them. He looked a little squeamish by the request but obliged when Hetorian nodded.

They continued their march up. They didn't know where they were going, but considering the attack was coming from the Haloti, it had to be up.

She spoke in a voice loud enough for all of them to hear. "Thank you for listening to me. If all goes as I hope, none of you will have to fire an arrow."

Several of the townspeople seemed pleased by this. "What happened at the temple?" Hetorian asked. "You seem infused and dead set on a specific goal."

"Yes, well, I hoped to deliver the news under better circumstances, but during my period of meditation, I was

The Final Offering

contacted by both Grimosias and Halothias together. They told me what I should do and that you should take up arms."

Gasps escaped the mouths of those behind her. She heard several mutterings but kept her mouth shut as she let them digest her news.

"I never expected anything like this to happen to you. No one has ever been contacted before. Normally I would question your word, but your appearance explains it all. But if they had a master plan why didn't they contact us directly?" Hetorian asked.

Explaining the reasoning provided to her, she hoped it settled the question. After all, she had no proof other than her word. She only hoped her short time spent with Hetorian was enough to convince him of her words and hoped his clout within the village would be enough to convince the rest of them. A sudden thought occurred to her as her mind settled on something he had mentioned a moment ago.

"Wait a minute, my appearance?" she asked. "What does my appearance have to do with anything?" She looked down at her clothes. They were the same ones she wore earlier in the day if not dirtier and wet with her sweat.

Hetorian looked stunned. "Your appearance is different," he said as if she should already know. "Your hair is bright white, when you left this morning it was dark brown. The skin of your face looks smoother, younger even," he paused. She started to speak, but he interrupted her. "And my goodness, Thula, your tattoos. This morning they were faint, and now they are bright; brighter and more colorful than I have ever seen. If I ever needed convincing the hand of God touch you, this would suffice." His voice filled with wonder.

She tried to look at her body to see what he referred to, but she would need a mirror for that. Grabbing a clump of hair in her hand, she brought it forward. The hair felt similar; like it always had, but sure as day, it was white. Dismay crossed her face as she tried to sort through it—a difficult task while running and climbing so many stairs.

As she surveyed her surroundings, she saw a group of Haloti waiting for them on the next branch. She couldn't make out who it was, but it only looked like eight troops. She signaled to the forty or so Grimmox and pointed to the branch. Several more ran to catch up with them on the next bough down.

They climbed the last flight of stairs and slowed to a walk, approaching the eight raised bows pointing at them. Thula took the lead.

As she walked forward, she wasn't at all surprised by the person standing in front. Of course, it was Amridon's unit. She recognized the rest of his troops; they had spent eight months together after all.

Be brave, she told herself. *You have to do this. It's what is right and what the sons of God have asked of you.* She took a deep breath.

"Amridon! Why am I not surprised you're leading the charge?" she asked.

Many blank and confused stares greeted her, but their bows never wavered. She stopped ten paces short of Amridon's position, recognizing the cold stare gazing back at her. She

The Final Offering

should have known. It was Amridon's body, but the hateful eyes staring at her belonged to none other than Silonia. Somehow, she used Amridon's body to communicate with her again, just as she had on the evening of their dinner.

"Thula!" he said in a guttural spit, filled with nothing but loathing. "I expected you to be dead by now; at least, that's what I ordered of the blue morpho butterfly who transported you here. How good it will be to finish you off once and for all."

Confusion filled the faces of the soldiers in Amridon's unit. They stared long and hard at her; it was as though they tried to decide if what he said was true. Several of them seemed to recognize her at the same time.

"We should have disposed of you when we had the chance, but the council had to vote against my decision." More bewildered looks from his troops. She even noticed when several of the bows lowered, even if only slightly.

"Why would you try attacking the Grimmox so soon after I left? You had to have known I would come down here and learn the truth." She spoke louder so everyone could hear. "But that's just it, isn't it? You expected the butterfly to finish me off, didn't you, Silonia?" She allowed the name to drawl across her tongue for emphasis.

"Bravo, the young one has connected all the dots. Not that it will do you any good when you're dead, and the rest of the filthy Grimmox are buried along with you." Shock filled the faces of several of the soldiers and one-by-one they lowered their bows. Amridon's body turned, distracted for just a moment. "What are you doing, you idiots? As the ranking soldier, I order you to raise your bows. On my mark…" His voice trailed off and his face contorted. "Thula? Is that really you?" Amridon spoke over Silonia and for a moment, she saw his brown eyes emerge from beneath the facade. It lasted but a second, but it was enough to give her hope.

She turned in a circle so she could address them all, noticing that hundreds more had arrived from both sides. This was the moment she waited for. Enough people had gathered to hear the truth. But could she do this? This thing they asked of her, all this pressure, what if she messed up?

"Struggling with my new role in Grimmox society, I went to the temple this morning for a period of meditation. I'd hoped to be guided to reason, but instead, Halothias and Grimosias contacted me." The murmurs and mutterings of the assembled crowd, both Grimmox and Haloti alike, helped her understand where everyone stood. Many of the Haloti who had just arrived realized who was speaking then and stared at her in fear as if she was resurrected from the grave.

Although the air was cool against her skin, sweat glistened on her forehead. She had never been comfortable speaking in front of crowds and the words she spoke today came from the sons of God, which only magnified her fears. This was *not* a message she could blunder.

"They spoke of many things," she turned to face the Haloti, "but most importantly, they told me how the elders have lied to us for centuries, to all of us. Lies that suited their own purposes."

Amridon's face filled with concern, but swiftly what looked like pure hatred and frustration claimed it again. If she didn't do

The Final Offering

something soon, he would, so she mustered up her courage and spoke on.

"The offering was our idea. It served the purpose of building trust with the Grimmox at the end of a long and bloody civil war. It was also a means to help repopulate the Grimmox village, while also serving as a deterrent from more wars, as now we would be one."

Continuing to turn as she spoke so everyone could hear her, she pressed on. "Grimosias and Halothias don't always agree, but they use words to solve their problems. None of this," she outstretched her arms for emphasis, "is what either of them ever wanted. Their father, our God, is angry and ready to teach us all a lesson by starting over. We have to work together if we will survive this."

Judging by the blank looks on many of their faces, she could tell she wasn't getting through to many of them and switched methods. "Can't you see the Haloti elders are using your fears against us to further their cause? Has anything they've done the past several months made any sense? Think about it. All they've done is aimed at building up the military. And for what, I ask you? So they could do exactly what they are doing today. For reasons I cannot fathom, they want the Grimmox eliminated. We're better than this and deserve more."

This wasn't all on the Haloti alone though, and she stopped so she faced the Grimmox. "You all have a part in this too. If someone is threatening you, it is your obligation to stand up and face down your attackers. Simply rolling over and accepting death is never a solution in the eyes of our Gods."

She heard the familiar twang of a released string of a bow. Something penetrated her flesh with enough force to spin her around. Heat filled the wound as pain spread through her body. She blinked her eyes in confusion as screams filled the air. Blood spilled from the wound and she gasped for breath as her body collided with the ground. In her last moments of consciousness, she saw Amridon's face contort once again, as a battle ensued within his head. She saw his eyes return to his own, and grief filled his face as he realized what he had done before her vision went black.

The Final Offering

Chapter 17

Thula blinked her eyes and tried to focus. Several of her friends from the espionage program filled her blurry vision. As their faces came into view, she saw the anguish on Hetorian's face as he bent over her. She tried to sit up among her concerned visitors, but a sharp pain shot up her left arm and she winced.

"You were shot with an arrow," Hetorian said. "Sit still until we get a medic up here."

"But Amridon, where is Amridon?" she asked.

Hetorian seemed a little hurt by her concern over her former love. "He's being held," he nodded over his shoulder.

She turned her head in the direction he pointed, careful not to further damage her injury. Amridon knelt on the branch and two Grimmox guards held him in place. His head lay forward, and tears streamed down his face.

A slight smile spread across her lips. "Good! He's weak minded and easily manipulated. Who knows what further damage he could create?" She spat on the ground with disgust as she turned and looked at Hetorian, a move that sent a pain shooting up her arm. "Was there any further attack? Please tell me everyone else is safe... that I succeeded in what they asked of me."

Hetorian tried to hide a grin but was unsuccessful. She saw right through it. "There was no other attack. Just the lone arrow Amridon—should I say Silonia—fired at you. You have succeeded." He kissed her forehead and smiled. "You really communicated with them? I can't believe it."

"Yes. I couldn't myself." She smiled through the pain but realized she couldn't finish telling her story. "I thought it was just a dream when I first regained consciousness. I had no idea they had altered my appearance. I guess I needed the help to convince you."

"What else did they tell you? Does it agree with what I've been teaching you this past week?" he asked.

"I'll get to all of that, but now is not the time. We still have much work before us," she said.

The Final Offering

As if right on cue, two soldiers arrived with alcohol and bandages. They cleaned and wrapped her wound. The cleaning hurt far worse than the wound felt before they arrived, but she gritted her teeth through it.

***

Over the next three days, she remained in bed to recover. Given the initial pain which only increased when she tried to move her fingers, she thought she would lose her arm. But the medics assured her full mobility would return, and sure enough, on day three she moved her fingers with only a slight lingering pain.

Someone knocked on the door and she sat up. Hetorian peaked his head inside the room and she invited him in from the comfort of her bed.

"How are you feeling?" he asked. "You seem to have more energy."

"I'm doing much better now that you're here." She grinned. Something about him seemed to pull her in as though she belonged in the warm embrace of his arms. "What happened to Amridon?"

"He's now locked away. We had to clear out the cells to make room for him." He walked forward and brushed several rogue strands of hair away from her eyes. "He'll be tried for attempted murder."

A small patter of pain worked its way through her stomach as she nodded in understanding. This isn't what she wanted at all, but it was most likely what would have to happen. Even if she no longer loved him, this wasn't the ending she had in mind.

Hetorian looked at her with concern. "Are you ready to tell me everything else you learned in your vision?"

She offered a coy smile. "I'd like to tell you, but I think it would be best if I revealed it to everyone all at once." She paused before shifting to other matters. "Has everything been set for the dinner?"

Hetorian informed her the previous day that the Grimmox wished to offer her a medal for her brave deed. With a few demands of her own, she reluctantly agreed.

"Yes. Everything is set for three nights from tonight," he said. Disappointment crept on to his face. He obviously had hoped to get more information from her.

***

Finally, the night arrived. With the help of Charlonne, she adorned a bright blue, silk gown and prepared for the dinner. Her arm still offered a small twinge of pain, but she bore it with little issue.

They headed down to the village square where an extravagant array of tables and food was set out. A large smile crossed her face when she noticed not only the Grimmox in attendance but also the entire Haloti village as well. The elders were not there, which brought her even more joy.

At her appearance, her mother, father, and sisters all stood and ran over to her, offering her hugs, and filling her face with kisses. She assured them she was fine, and after several rushed moments of disbelief at seeing their precious daughter again, delight at embracing her, and shock at what she was called to do, they returned to their table. Hetorian arrived to escort her to

The Final Offering

the seat of honor. Several members of the Grimmox council sat with her as did Governor Linotas and Assistant Governor Mycell of the Haloti. She smiled at them as she took her seat.

The dinner was several courses and concluded with the best Thornberry pie she had ever tasted. With their stomachs stuffed and spoke.

"I would like to thank the fine members of the Haloti village who attended tonight's ceremony. It brings me much joy to have so many of your faces with us this evening." A round of applause filled the cool evening air. She turned to Thula and said, "We've put aside our differences—for one evening at least—to honor the heroic deeds of Thula. She staved off a war and suffered a grave injury to put a stop to our madness. Thula, we would like to offer this medal as a small token of our appreciation." She bent forward and put it around her neck. "This can never take away your injury, but I hope it shows a little of our appreciation for all you've done." Tremon smiled.

It was her time to speak, and dread almost overcame her. "Thank you, Tremon," she said in a wavering voice. "I only did what we deemed necessary." She saw the confusion spread through the crowd at the mention of we.

Taking a deep breath, she began. "On the morning of the Haloti's attempted attack, I went to the temple for meditation. I was skeptical of what may happen, but Halothias and Grimosias contacted me. They stood before me and offered the full truth. For the first time, in a long time, I felt as though I truly understood our history."

She continued, sharing all the brothers revealed to her. Many in the crowd looked confused and seemed to question her words. She tried to put those to the side. "I was as skeptical as you appear to be now. Any who saw me before that morning would know I went through a dramatic transformation, emotionally and physically. In their infinite wisdom, the brothers changed my outward appearance, without even letting me know. It seems it was the perfect piece of the puzzle to show those closest to me, what I spoke was the truth.

"The time has come for us to put our differences aside. We are all one and the same; from the same seed, and the same beginnings." She paused. "We are all brothers and sisters and we should act like it. We may have different skin and we may have different beliefs, but do we not all serve the same God? Do we not all have the same markings adorning our bodies, the same blue blood, pumping through our veins?"

She took a moment to think for herself, before continuing. "If I have learned anything, it's that we are allowed to disagree. While we're all the same, we're all individuals with different thoughts and ideas. Sure, we won't always be on the same page, but as I saw, even Halothias and Grimosias couldn't agree on everything." She smiled thinking of the eternal brothers doing just that during their time with her. "But did they try to kill one another because they didn't get along? No! They agreed to disagree and worked it out amongst themselves...with words, not weapons.

"It's time we do the same. Follow the lead of our ancestors, where we work together for the betterment of our society. We need to trust one another and work together. There's a lot we can learn from each other, which is the way it was meant to be."

She looked around the room. "I understand the Haloti have already taken the first step and have imprisoned the elders. No

The Final Offering

more shall they reign supreme, and I commend you for your efforts. It's not easy, but it's the right move.

"The time has arrived for us to think for ourselves. The days of living in fear are over, and the real healing can finally begin." Thunderous applause filled the gathering as people rose to their feet to show their support.

"I'm not up here to preach to you, or to tell you how to think. That is for you to decide, but nobody will stand in the way of your beliefs, nor is it okay for us to stand in the way of anyone else's. So join me, join your brothers and sisters, as we work to begin a society where everyone is equal. Where no one is judged based on their beliefs, or their skin color. It is time to put those petty biases and judgments aside. Embrace one another for who we all are; which is fairies of the same tree."

Many in attendance jumped to their feet. Birds flew out of the cedar tree from the sudden cacophony permeating the air. She let it die down before she concluded.

"Before I leave—many of you must be tired—I have one further request. I wish to have Amridon released from any and all charges." She paused as she heard shocked mutterings and hushed whispers whip through the crowd. "He wasn't acting on his own behalf, but rather under the control of Elder Silonia. The soldiers who were with me on that day can verify that he even responded to the name Silonia when I confronted him. While he harbors some hatred toward the Grimmox, he is a man of reason. It will take time, but I'm sure he will embrace the newfound peace suggested this evening."

She sat back down amid further applause. There would be some who disagreed with what she presented, but given her current position, she only hoped they would come around.

***

The days and years that followed weren't easy. It's never easy when everything you believe in is thrown into upheaval, but as the generations passed, so too did the previous prejudices. Thula and Hetorian were eventually sealed, and they had five children together. At the time of her death in her eighty-second year, she was blessed with fourteen grandchildren. Amridon found love in the form of who else, a Grimmox.

As Thula predicted, the road to peace was fraught with tumultuous times. Eventually, it became a story passed down through the generations, passed down through their beloved tree, and served as a lesson to any who had ideas to stray.

The Final Offering

If you enjoyed this book, please write a review on Amazon HERE

If you're unsure of what to include in a review, I have attached a cheat sheet on the next page.

Check out my Fantasy Series, The Keepers of the Orbs and other writing project by visiting
http://www.jggatewood.com

Book 1: The Unknown Man

J.G. Gatewood

Book 2: The Rising Past

Book 3: A Shadow Within

The Final Offering

Coming Soon in Early 2018, my Adult

Urban Fantasy Novel, Vampire's Curse

And due out the end of 2018 is the

conclusion to the Keepers of the Orbs Series

J.G. Gatewood

J.G. Gatewood lives in Parker, CO with his wife, Sarah, and two sons, Branden and Evan. When not writing, he works as a Subject Matter Expert. He enjoys sports and reading in his free time. For more information, please visit http://www.jggatewood.com

Printed in Great Britain
by Amazon